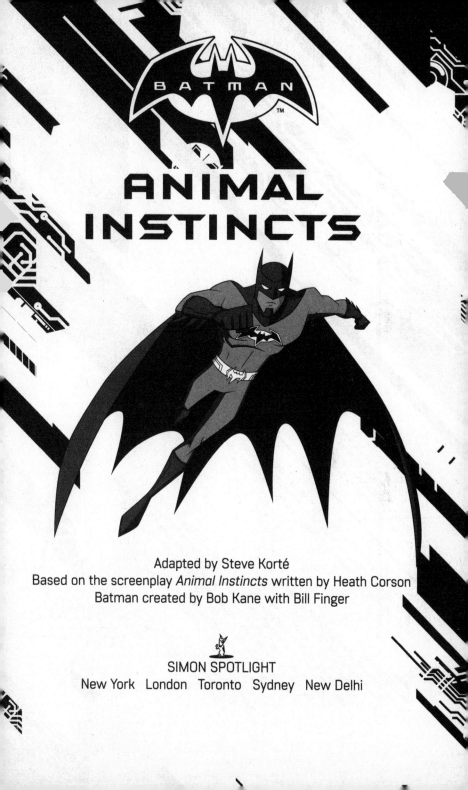

BATMAN™

ANIMAL INSTINCTS

Adapted by Steve Korté
Based on the screenplay *Animal Instincts* written by Heath Corson
Batman created by Bob Kane with Bill Finger

SIMON SPOTLIGHT
New York   London   Toronto   Sydney   New Delhi

Based on the screenplay written by Heath Corson

Copyright © 2016 DC Comics.

BATMAN and all related characters and elements © & ™ DC Comics and
Warner Bros. Entertainment Inc. (s16)

SIMON SPOTLIGHT
An imprint of Simon & Schuster Children's Publishing Division
1230 Avenue of the Americas, New York, New York 10020
This Simon Spotlight hardcover edition August 2016
All rights reserved, including the right of reproduction in whole or in part in any form.
SIMON SPOTLIGHT and colophon are registered trademarks of Simon & Schuster, Inc.
For information about special discounts for bulk purchases, please contact Simon & Schuster
Special Sales at 1-866-506-1949 or business@simonandschuster.com.
Designed by Nicholas Sciacca
The text of this book was set in Core Sans.
Manufactured in the United States of America 0716 FFG
10 9 8 7 6 5 4 3 2 1
ISBN 978-1-4814-7732-1 (hc)
ISBN 978-1-4814-7731-4 (pbk)
ISBN 978-1-4814-7733-8 (eBook)

CHAPTER 1

The sky over Gotham City was growing darker as night approached. Businesspeople left their office buildings and flooded into the subway stations, eager to get home from work. Others darted between stores, finishing up the last of their shopping before the evening rush was in full swing. Still, they all knew to stay as far as possible from the dimly lit alleys where criminals often lurked. Even the members of the Gotham City Police Department walked cautiously through the city's streets after the sun went down.

Despite the best efforts of the police, Gotham City's

criminals were always finding new ways to outsmart the law. Police hovercrafts floated above the buildings. Occasionally, a bright spotlight would shine from above, illuminating the inky black streets below in search of trouble.

Skyscrapers towered high above the bustling streets of downtown Gotham City, and along those buildings were dozens of bright neon signs and video screens. The largest video screen was almost fifty feet tall and covered the side of a building. The evening news was being broadcast on that screen, and a young newscaster smiled with excitement as she spoke. Behind her was an animated image of a giant asteroid flying through outer space.

"There are just three more days until Gotham City will be able to spot the passage of Midas Heart, the asteroid with a solid gold core that passes the Earth every seventy-seven years," she said.

The screen then switched to an image of an unusual-looking man who was wearing a tuxedo and an old-fashioned top hat. He had a long, sharp nose and wore a monocle in his right eye.

The newscaster continued, "And finally, tonight is the grand opening of the Aviary, Gotham City's newest and tallest building. Count on high society to flock to Oswald Cobblepot's *very* exclusive opening-night celebration."

A police hovercraft floated quietly past the video screen. Inside the craft, two policemen were dressed in combat gear. The dispatcher from police headquarters came over the radio as they piloted the craft higher.

"Go ahead, four-oh-nine. What's your status?"

"All clear from up here, dispatch," one of the policemen said. "Re-engaging for another pass."

The dispatcher's voice crackled over the communicator in response. "Roger that, four-oh-nine." There was a pause, and then she spoke in almost a whisper. "Hey, Tony . . . have you seen him tonight?"

"Sorry, buddy, not tonight," the policeman said as he peered through the windows of the hovercraft. "No sign of the Batman."

"All right. Let me know if you do, huh?" she said.

As the hovercraft glided over the skyline, a dark figure moved within the shadows atop one building. The figure waited until the police vehicle was out of sight, and then he stepped forward into the moonlight. It was Batman, the masked crime fighter who prowled the streets and rooftops of Gotham City in search of criminals. During the day, Batman was secretly Bruce Wayne, CEO of Wayne

Enterprises and one of the world's wealthiest men. In the evening, he became Batman, the Dark Knight of Gotham City. He was not only a skilled fighter, but also a master detective.

Batman moved to the ledge of the building and fired his grapple launcher.

WHOOSH!

A long metal cord with a sharp hook at the end shot out of the device. The hook lodged itself into a nearby building, and within seconds Batman was swinging through the air, his fist holding tightly on to the cord and his black cape flowing behind him.

Just as Batman was about to crash into the next building over, he released his hand from the cord and extended his cape into two flexible glider wings, allowing him to sail silently through the air. As he soared high above Gotham, he scanned the city streets below for any signs of trouble.

PING!

Batman received an electronic alert on the communicator device on his cowl. It was Alfred, the trusted butler of Bruce Wayne. Alfred also served as one of Batman's most devoted assistants.

"Yes, Alfred?" asked Batman.

"I had a question that simply could not wait, sir," said Alfred.

Batman effortlessly flew over the building rooftops, remaining in the shadows as much as possible and avoiding the glare of the bright neon lights and video screens below.

"Which is?" he said, urging Alfred to continue.

"I was inquiring as to which suit Bruce Wayne might need pressed for his meetings tomorrow."

Batman reached up to his cowl and tapped the area next to his right eye. With each tap, the lenses in his mask shifted from night vision to infrared to X-ray, allowing him to better scan the dark streets below.

"*That* was your question that couldn't wait?" Batman asked gruffly.

"These are the things that keep me up at night, Master Bruce," Alfred replied calmly.

Batman smiled as he adjusted his wings and banked high into the air.

"Was there anything else, Alfred?" Batman asked.

"I was inquiring how much longer your patrol would go on this evening. You see, I've cooked coq au vin." Alfred sighed.

There was a long pause as Batman adjusted his

scanners. Something was going on at S.T.A.R. Labs, the laboratory complex downtown.

"Looks like I'll be late. I've got work to do," said Batman as he shifted position and started his descent toward the center of Gotham City.

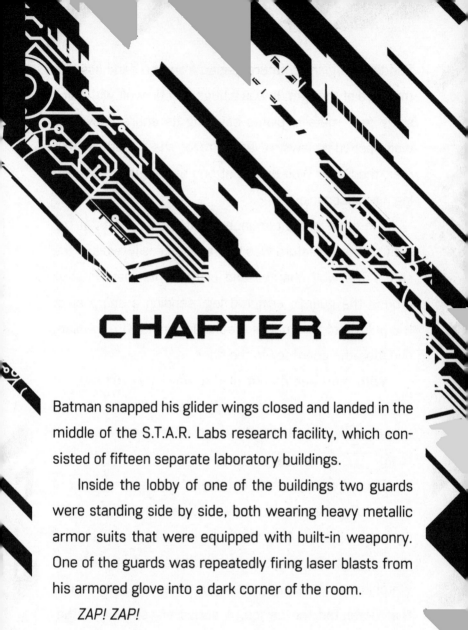

CHAPTER 2

Batman snapped his glider wings closed and landed in the middle of the S.T.A.R. Labs research facility, which consisted of fifteen separate laboratory buildings.

Inside the lobby of one of the buildings two guards were standing side by side, both wearing heavy metallic armor suits that were equipped with built-in weaponry. One of the guards was repeatedly firing laser blasts from his armored glove into a dark corner of the room.

ZAP! ZAP!

There was silence. As the guards watched nervously, a pair of animal eyes slowly blinked in the shadows.

Suddenly, a giant creature leaped from the darkness into the glare of the light. It was a huge robotic wolf with thick shiny gray metallic plates covering its entire body. The wolf opened its jaws, revealing razor-sharp teeth. With a roar, the Cyber Wolf lunged at one of the guards, knocking him unconscious.

The other guard continued to fire laser blasts at the wolf, but the creature was too fast and easily avoided the shots. The wolf charged and clamped its metallic jaws around the guard's armored leg, sending a sharp electric pulse into the guard's mechanical suit. With a violent shudder, the guard fell to the floor.

With both guards out of the way, the wolf ran out of the lobby and down a complex labyrinth of hallways. It was as if the creature knew exactly where it wanted to go.

Soon the wolf arrived outside a room at the center of the building. Peering in, it saw a table with a bright spotlight shining on it. Atop the table was a large mechanical device, gleaming brightly. The wolf paused at the door, watching the constantly moving red laser security beams that protected the device. A series of complex mathematical calculations appeared within the wolf's eyes, and then the creature deftly jumped inside.

Just as one laser beam approached, the wolf executed a perfect backflip and hopped over the laser. The creature jumped, rolled, and slid around each beam. In seconds it had reached the middle of the room and was just about to grab the mechanical device.

BLAM!

A Batarang knocked the wolf to the ground. It looked up in surprise to see Batman standing by the door.

"That doesn't belong to you," Batman said as he quickly launched another series of Batarangs at the room's security system boxes. The boxes exploded from the impact, and suddenly, all of the red laser beams disappeared.

As Batman stepped into the room, the wolf quickly scanned him and all his weaponry. Then, judging the hero to be much stronger than itself, it rolled its head back and opened its mouth wide. A sturdy metallic cable shot out of the wolf's mouth and knocked a hole in the ceiling. Before Batman could reach the creature, it was pulled aloft by the cable and disappeared.

Batman quickly fired a grapple and followed the mechanical monster onto the rooftop. The wolf scrambled across the buildings, jumping from one to another, but Batman was close behind, matching the robot move for move.

Soon, Batman and the Cyber Wolf were at the edge of the S.T.A.R. Labs complex, near an entrance to the Gotham City Highway. The wolf was running out of rooftops. The last one was just ahead, and it was much farther away than any of the others. The wolf quickly accelerated, running faster and faster, getting ready to make its biggest leap yet. With all its strength, the wolf launched itself into the air and grappled on to the faraway ledge. Seconds later a Batarang soared through the air and made contact with the building just below the mechanical creature's grip. The Batarang started beeping, and then—

BOOM!

The Batarang bomb destroyed the ledge of the building, and the robotic wolf was sent crashing down four stories. With a thud, the creature landed on its back in the middle of the highway. Calmly, the wolf got back on its feet. There wasn't a scratch on it.

A man inside a car twisted his steering wheel and swerved to avoid hitting the robot. Just then, Batman jumped from the building and landed next to the wolf.

With a snarl, the wolf leaped to the opposite side of the highway. Batman pursued, dodging cars as he ran against the flow of traffic. The wolf pounced onto a large oncoming semitruck that was barreling right toward

Batman. The driver of the truck was frantically pushing on the brake, but there wasn't enough time to stop. Just as the truck was about to hit him, Batman threw himself down to the ground and rolled out of the way.

SCREEEECH!

The truck had toppled over and was skidding down the highway, throwing sparks everywhere. When it finally came to a stop, the driver crawled out of the truck and looked around with a stunned expression.

"What the heck was—?!" he started to say. "Whoa! It's Batman!"

As the other drivers started to emerge from their cars, Batman scanned the area, but the mechanical wolf had escaped. And if Batman wanted to find it, he was going to need help.

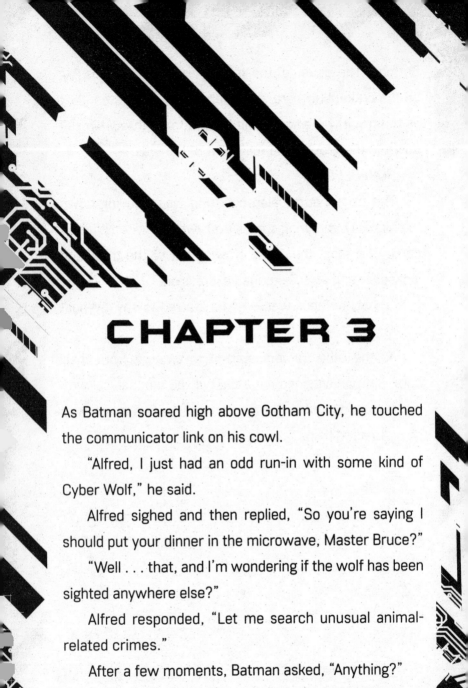

CHAPTER 3

As Batman soared high above Gotham City, he touched the communicator link on his cowl.

"Alfred, I just had an odd run-in with some kind of Cyber Wolf," he said.

Alfred sighed and then replied, "So you're saying I should put your dinner in the microwave, Master Bruce?"

"Well . . . that, and I'm wondering if the wolf has been sighted anywhere else?"

Alfred responded, "Let me search unusual animal-related crimes."

After a few moments, Batman asked, "Anything?"

"Nothing with wolves, but there seems to be an uptick of late in cat burglaries."

Batman frowned as he headed back to do another sweep of the area. Cat burglaries were all too often connected to his longtime foe, Catwoman.

Across town Nightwing, one of Batman's most valued crime-fighting allies, was investigating a break-in at the Belle and the Bird jewelry store. Nightwing was also an expert in martial arts and almost as talented a detective as Batman.

"Looks like someone skipped their catnap to swipe some jewels," Nightwing said as he arrived on the scene.

Inside the darkened store a stealthy figure had just crawled through a broken window and was slowly moving toward a glass display case filled with diamond jewelry.

CRACK!

The intruder shattered the glass case and grabbed a handful of necklaces.

"Pretty, shiny, and sparkling," she said with a purr. "All my favorite things!"

As she fingered the jewels and walked back toward the window, a voice called out.

"Hold it right there, Catwoman!" yelled Nightwing as

he tumbled through the window and into the store.

But as Nightwing landed on his feet, he was astonished to see that he was not facing Catwoman. Instead a ferocious half-woman, half-feline villain named Cheetah was baring her sharp claws at him. Cheetah possessed superstrength and was able to strike with amazing speed, making her a formidable opponent.

"What's your problem, Nightwing?" she taunted. "Gotham City only big enough for *one* cat-lady? You'll make me insecure."

"Why? You should know by now that nobody likes a *cheetah*."

"Aww. Come over here, and we can *hiss* and make up."

Nightwing raised one of his electric-powered batons and twirled it rapidly. He was about to throw the baton at Cheetah, but she lunged at him, knocking him off-balance. His baton clattered to the floor. Cheetah's claws were fully extended as she launched one vicious swipe after another at Nightwing. He expertly twisted his body to avoid her dangerous claws.

Cheetah smiled and jumped onto Nightwing's back, pinning him to the ground with her knees on his shoulders. With all his strength, Nightwing strained to reach his baton. Just as Cheetah's claws were about to scratch his face, Nightwing grabbed the baton and activated the electronic pulse. The baton delivered a crackling electric shock that sent Cheetah rocketing backward against the wall.

"Shocking, right?" Nightwing said with a grin. "You know, it's okay if you just want to surrender now."

Cheetah looked up at Nightwing and narrowed her eyes.

"You didn't really think I came here all by myself, did you?" she said.

RUMMMMMMBLE!

The ground shook, and the display cases in the jewelry store started swaying. Something big was approaching. Just then, the floor was cracked open by a giant fist. Nightwing looked on in dismay as the massive reptilian monster known as Killer Croc crawled into the room. His scaly green skin glistened with water from the Gotham City sewers. At a height of seven feet, five inches and weighing 686 pounds, Killer Croc was incredibly strong and easily angered. He was also one of Gotham City's most dangerous villains.

"Aw, you started without me?" Killer Croc complained to Cheetah.

"I can't wait all night for you to haul your scaly butt out of the sewer, Croc," replied Cheetah with a yawn. "Nightwing, you know Croc."

"Oh yeah. We've met," Croc said.

"You've thickened up, though, haven't you?" said Nightwing. "Maybe you should cut out snacks before bed."

Furious, Croc came at Nightwing swinging his gigantic fists, one of which punched clean through a display case. Still, the hero managed to dodge most of Croc's punches until Cheetah jumped into the fight, kicking Nightwing from behind.

"Finish the mission. I'll take care of him," Killer Croc grumbled as he pulled himself to his full height, towering over Nightwing. Cheetah darted from the room.

Killer Croc let out a furious roar and swung his huge arms once more, trying to land a deadly punch. Nightwing dodged left and right, staying just out of Croc's reach. Then Nightwing reached for his electric baton and hurled it at Croc, but it barely missed him and hit the jewelry store's security system box instead.

"That'll work," Nightwing said with a grin. There was a loud electric crackle, and suddenly, the security system was activated. Bright lights flooded the store, and a siren started wailing.

Cheetah ran back into the room and knocked Nightwing to the ground with his other baton before jumping onto Croc's shoulders.

"The job is done," she whispered to Croc.

"Let's scram before Batman shows up," Croc growled.

Just as Croc was about to crash through a wall and escape, a bright red blur surrounded him.

ZZZZZZZIP!

"Leaving?" the blur asked, coming to a halt. "But I just got here!" Suddenly, The Flash was standing in front of Killer Croc and Cheetah. Covered from head to toe in a form-fitting red uniform, The Flash was the Fastest Man Alive and a longtime friend of Batman and his allies . . . well, *most* of his allies.

"Great. What are *you* doing here?" Nightwing asked with a frown.

"I've been tracking Croc since he robbed the Central City copper quarry last week."

Croc and Cheetah tried to slip away while the heroes chatted, but The Flash ran fast enough around them that there was nowhere to go—everywhere they looked, multiple versions of The Flash were surrounding them!

"I got hit harder than I thought," Nightwing mumbled. "I'm seeing five of you."

"It's cool, right?" The Flash said, suddenly back at Nightwing's side.

"Nope. Not even a little," Nightwing grumbled as The Flash tried to help him to his feet. "I don't need your help. I was doing fine."

"Is that why you tripped the alarm?" asked The Flash with a smile. "With me here, we can wrap this up *quickly*!"

The Flash jumped into action, circling Killer Croc with hundreds of punches at superspeed.

"I didn't think it was possible, but you're even uglier up close," The Flash said to Croc. "But that's nothing compared to the smell. When's the last time you bathed, dude? Never? I mean, I *get* it. You're a giant walking, talking crocodile. But have some standards, man!"

"That kinda tickles. How about this?" Killer Croc said as he extended his massive arm. Croc's scaly forearm caught The Flash right in his stomach.

BLAM!

The Flash fell to the ground, clutching his stomach in pain. Cheetah darted over to join the action, but Nightwing stopped her. "Uh-uh-uh—we never finished our dance."

Nightwing moved to strike, but Cheetah was faster. She knocked him to the ground and then threw him across the room where The Flash was still down for the count. As the two heroes slowly staggered to their feet, the villains escaped.

"They're gone," said Nightwing.

The Flash jumped up and began zipping around the jewelry store, peering under cases, looking behind doors, and even peeking under the rug.

"Yeah, they're gone all right," he reported.

"Thanks for the update," said Nightwing sarcastically. "Batman should know about this."

"That was a weird team-up, wasn't it?" The Flash asked as Nightwing walked away.

"Them? Or us?" Nightwing snapped.

"Touché," The Flash said with a grin.

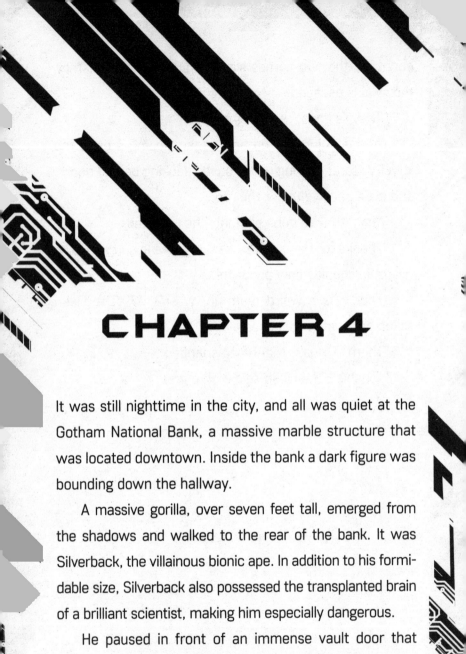

CHAPTER 4

It was still nighttime in the city, and all was quiet at the Gotham National Bank, a massive marble structure that was located downtown. Inside the bank a dark figure was bounding down the hallway.

A massive gorilla, over seven feet tall, emerged from the shadows and walked to the rear of the bank. It was Silverback, the villainous bionic ape. In addition to his formidable size, Silverback also possessed the transplanted brain of a brilliant scientist, making him especially dangerous.

He paused in front of an immense vault door that was protected by a high-tech security system. Silverback activated his electronic eyepiece to scan the vault's security and smiled, pulling out a pocket-size computer in front of the door. The computer made clicking noises as it scrolled through millions of numbers to determine the vault's password. Ten seconds later the light on the security door changed from red to green.

Silverback turned the latch on the vault, opened it, and stepped inside. He was now standing in front of hundreds of rows of glittering silver bars. "Checkpoint complete," he said into his earpiece. "Initiating next phase." Silverback grinned as he started sliding the silver bars into a large duffel bag.

WHOOOSH!

An arrow ripped through the air, slicing the bottom of the bag. The silver bars tumbled onto the floor.

"What happened?!" the giant ape exclaimed, examining the bag.

Silverback spun around to find a masked man wearing a green outfit. It was Green Arrow, the crime fighter and expert archer. He was also highly skilled at hand-to-hand combat.

"A talking gorilla robbing a bank? Now I've seen everything," said Green Arrow as he nocked another arrow to his bowstring.

"Aah, *Green Arrow* happened. I'll have to remedy that."

"I get it," Green Arrow said, examining Silverback. He bore a remarkable resemblance to another one of Green Arrow's foes. "You're like Gorilla Grod *lite*. All the gorilla, none of the brains."

"*I* am Silverback. *You* are toast!" yelled the ape as he raised both arms and pointed them at Green Arrow. He aimed the lasers that were mounted on his wrist gauntlets and opened fire.

Green Arrow ducked to avoid the laser beams that shot over him. He quickly rolled for cover behind a large mahogany desk.

Green Arrow removed an arrow from his quiver and fired it to land just in front of Silverback. Thick black smoke started to billow from the arrow and rapidly filled the room.

"That's my special smokescreen arrow," the hero announced. "Patent pending."

"Your smoke is immaterial," Silverback said with disgust. "Switching to heat sensor!"

"Wait, what, now?" asked a puzzled Green Arrow.

Silverback's bionic eyepiece switched to its heat sensor mode. The giant ape could now easily see Green

Arrow through the smoke and resumed firing lasers at him. One laser blast sliced through the desk in front of the hero, almost hitting him.

"That didn't go the way I expected," Green Arrow said, taking cover once more.

Batman was still scanning the skies over Gotham City when he received a distress call from Nightwing. "What happened?" he asked.

"I don't know—something weird. I'm uploading the footage to your subnet now."

Inside his cowl Batman watched the replay footage of The Flash and Nightwing's fight against Cheetah and Killer Croc. He was stunned. "Croc and Cheetah working together? That's new."

"I figured you'd want to know," Nightwing said as he somersaulted onto a nearby ledge.

"And The Flash, he mentioned a copper quarry," Batman continued, thinking aloud. "That's not Croc's MO."

"Maybe it's the Midas asteroid passing the Earth, making everyone crazy."

But before Batman could say any more, another call came through: It was Alfred. "I'm afraid I have yet another animal-related crime, and it's in progress as we speak," he said in a rush, sending Batman the coordinates for Gotham National Bank.

Batman frowned. "I'm on my way. Nightwing, see if you can track where Cheetah and Croc snuck off to."

Green Arrow rolled and jumped again, dodging the laser blasts that continued to bombard him. Silverback was proving to be a more difficult opponent than he'd anticipated. The hero was exhausted and running out of ideas. He ran behind a small marble pillar, reached into his quiver, and, firing from memory, shot two arrows into the dense smoke cloud that covered Silverback.

One arrow headed directly for Silverback, but the ape easily dodged before it could connect. The other arrow, though, found its target and smashed directly into the barrel of one of Silverback's wrist lasers.

BAM!

The wrist laser exploded, and Silverback cried out. "Impossible! No one could make that shot."

"Impossible is my middle name!" gloated Green Arrow. "Actually," he continued under his breath, "my middle name is Jonas, but I'm not telling *you* that." But he didn't have long to enjoy his victory. Silverback pounded his chest and let out a mighty roar, charging toward Green

Arrow. The hero shot a grappling arrow up onto one of the higher floors and, once positioned, aimed at Silverback from above. Before the hero could shoot again, Silverback began to climb up to him. He fired off one, two, three arrows, but Silverback swatted them away.

Suddenly, the shadow of a giant bat fell over the floor.

Green Arrow let out a sigh of relief. "You're a sight for sore eyes, Batman."

Silverback looked up with an evil grin and said, "You have it backward. Meet Man-Bat!"

SHREEEEEEEEEK!

From above came a bloodcurdling screech. A man-size bat swooped down from the ceiling, giant wings extended and razor-sharp claws glinting in the light. The creature was covered in fur, and its fiery red eyes glared at Green Arrow as it dove toward him. One of Man-Bat's claws pierced the hero's shoulder, knocking him off balance. Silverback grabbed the archer, slamming him to the ground, then lifted the hero as though he weighed nothing.

"We are the Animilitia!"

"The whaaaat?" said Green Arrow with disbelief. "More like the Zoo Crew!"

"Mock us if you must," shouted Silverback, "but you will *not* stop us!"

"Maybe not," Arrow began, "but *he* will."

Batman swung through an open window and rappelled down from above, delivering a swift kick to Silverback's face that sent the ape flying.

"Use your sonic-tip arrow to scramble Man-Bat's sonar," Batman said as he headed for Silverback.

"On it!" yelled Green Arrow as he loaded an arrow into his bow and launched it. The arrow emitted a loud pulsing sound, which caused Man-Bat to grab his ears in pain. The creature swerved wildly around the room, clearly unable to navigate, before crashing to the ground.

Seeing Batman coming toward him, Silverback hurled a desk at the hero. "Enough. We accomplished what we came for," Silverback said to Man-Bat. "Activating backup."

Silverback crouched down and then catapulted himself into the air, trying to make a run for it. Batman hurled bolas at the villain, which tied his legs together, causing him to collapse with an audible thud. Man-Bat swerved in the air to make another pass at the heroes, but was intercepted by one of Green Arrow's boxing-glove arrows.

Batman flung a Batarang to finish Silverback off, but just then a giant robotic tiger leaped through the window, landing inches away from him. It was soon followed by a large Cyber Bat that swooped around the room, shooting lasers from its eyes.

"What is *that*?" asked Green Arrow.

"Their backup," said Batman as he reached into his Utility Belt and withdrew an electro-Batarang. He skillfully launched it so that the Batarang lodged itself between two metal panels on the tiger.

ZZZZZZZAAAAP!

A powerful charge of electricity coursed through the mechanical tiger, but it kept moving. As the heroes continued to pummel the Cyber Animals, Man-Bat and Silverback made their escape.

Longing to go after them, Green Arrow landed an explosive arrow on the robotic bat, but it sailed through the explosion with only slight damage. Then, as quickly as they'd appeared, both Cyber Animals fled through the window.

Green Arrow rubbed the bruise on his shoulder. "Tell me, Bats—is it a full moon? Or is every night in Gotham City this weird?"

There was no answer. Batman had disappeared.

"I *hate* it when he does that," said Green Arrow.

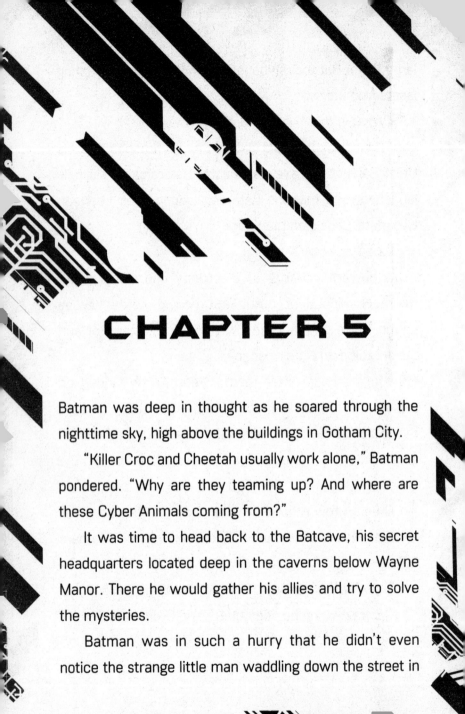

CHAPTER 5

Batman was deep in thought as he soared through the nighttime sky, high above the buildings in Gotham City.

"Killer Croc and Cheetah usually work alone," Batman pondered. "Why are they teaming up? And where are these Cyber Animals coming from?"

It was time to head back to the Batcave, his secret headquarters located deep in the caverns below Wayne Manor. There he would gather his allies and try to solve the mysteries.

Batman was in such a hurry that he didn't even notice the strange little man waddling down the street in one of the roughest parts of town. The man was Oswald Cobblepot, one of the wealthiest men in the world. He was impeccably dressed in a tuxedo coat that had a thick fur collar. His right eye squinted behind a monocle, and he jauntily twirled his umbrella as he walked past three young men who were gathered on a stoop outside a convenience store. The men were munching on groceries they had stolen just a few minutes earlier.

"Evening, gentlemen," said Cobblepot as he tipped his hat in front of the glaring men.

"Hey, get a load of this weirdo in his fancy clothes," said one of them with a harsh laugh.

"I bet he's got some extra money in his wallet that he doesn't need!" said another as he jumped off the stoop and moved menacingly toward Cobblepot.

"Ah, humanity," said Cobblepot with a sigh as he turned to face them. "You never fail to disappoint me."

"Hey guys, turns out he talks as funny as he looks," said the young man standing next to Cobblepot. "How about if you hand over your wallet, you old . . ."

"Gentlemen, I recall when I too was blind to the precariousness of human nature, unaware that with the slightest nudge, the world could crash down around me," Cobblepot said as he squeezed his right eye tightly around his monocle, which activated an X-ray camera within the eyepiece and allowed him to scan the building behind the hoodlums. With a smile, he detected a thin crack within a metal support railing that held up a brick balcony. Cobblepot tapped his umbrella against the railing, causing the crack to widen.

SNAP!

The balcony swayed, causing several bricks to loosen and fall to the ground.

CLUNK!

One brick landed with a crash on top of the would-be thief. The man fell to the ground, unconscious.

"Sweet dreams, young man," said Cobblepot.

"Nobody does that to my cousin!" yelled one of the men as both he and his companion launched themselves at Cobblepot.

Barely even glancing at his assailants, Cobblepot expertly swung his umbrella, landing a hard blow to the stomach of one. The handle of the umbrella then wrapped around the ankle of the other man, sending him crashing into a nearby garbage can. All three hoodlums now lay crumpled on the ground, none of them moving.

"Thank you for the exercise, gentlemen," said Cobblepot. "I found it quite bracing!"

With that, he tipped his hat again and waddled across the street to the Aviary Building, an immense skyscraper that was almost completely dark. Cobblepot hummed quietly with satisfaction as he rode the elevator to the basement, where he entered a large high-tech laboratory. There were three pulsing electronic devices in the center of the room, each connected to a series of wires. Connected to those wires were the robotic wolf, tiger, and bat. They were the same three Cyber Animals that had attacked Batman and the other heroes. White-coated technicians and scientists were carefully examining the robots for any damage to their metallic bodies.

Cobblepot waddled over to the Cyber Tiger and patted its head.

"Welcome home, my pets," said Cobblepot. "I trust you had a successful night out."

The tiger roared in agreement.

"Excellent. You three have passed your tests with flying colors," said Cobblepot.

"Mr. Cobblepot," said a voice behind him. "May I speak with you, please?"

Cobblepot frowned as one of the scientists walked over to him. The man appeared very nervous as he approached Cobblepot. His hands were trembling.

"Mr. Cobblepot, allow me to renew my concerns about this evening's events," he said. "More research is needed before we allow these robots to roam freely through Gotham City. Field tests are one thing, but this seems to be something very different."

"I'm not having this conversation with you again, Dr. Langstrom," said Cobblepot angrily as he pointed the tip of his umbrella at the scientist's throat. "Power up the charging stations for the animals . . . now!"

Langstrom wearily waved his hand to the other technicians, and soon the charging stations sprang to life, sending electrical energy surging into the three Cyber Animals.

"There is just one more assignment for my pets, and we will have *all* of Gotham City at our feet," Cobblepot said with a sinister smile.

"Well, what's left of it, anyway. Wauk-wauk-wauk," he added, emitting a laugh that sounded more like a penguin's call.

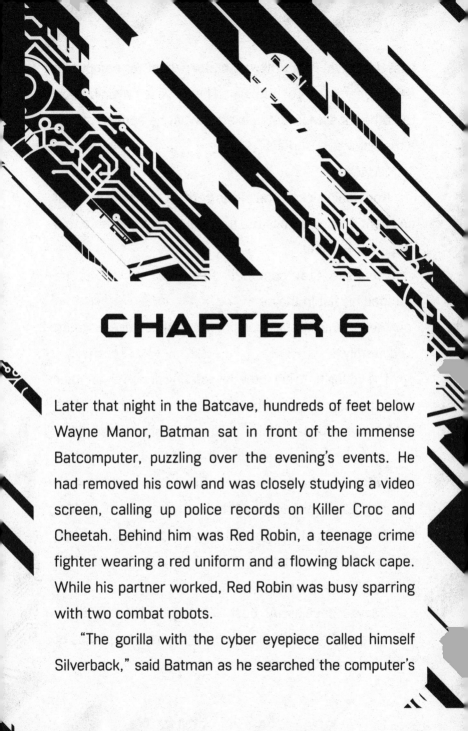

CHAPTER 6

Later that night in the Batcave, hundreds of feet below Wayne Manor, Batman sat in front of the immense Batcomputer, puzzling over the evening's events. He had removed his cowl and was closely studying a video screen, calling up police records on Killer Croc and Cheetah. Behind him was Red Robin, a teenage crime fighter wearing a red uniform and a flowing black cape. While his partner worked, Red Robin was busy sparring with two combat robots.

"The gorilla with the cyber eyepiece called himself Silverback," said Batman as he searched the computer's vast database, "but other than a penchant for computer-ized gadgets, I've got nothing on him. I've got even less on the other one. Man-Bat is exactly what he appears to be, a man-size bat. Curious."

SMACK!

Red Robin kicked one of the combat robots in its neck and sent it flying across the floor. The robot clattered to a stop near Batman.

"You see that combo?!" Red Robin yelled as he pumped his fist in the air.

"Yeah. You're still dropping your shoulder," Batman said sternly.

The young hero landed a devastating punch on another robot, causing it to stumble backward onto the first. "Red Robin saves the day again," said Red Robin with a smile.

Batman returned to the screen and said quietly to himself, "Elsewhere, reports of Killer Croc and Cheetah teaming up. Together they broke out of Arkham Asylum about three months ago and have committed five rob-beries together before tonight's jewelry store break-in. I believe they're related."

"Maybe cousins. At best," Red Robin offered as he peered over Batman's shoulder and studied the photos of Killer Croc and Cheetah.

"No, the crimes are related," Batman said with a sigh.

"Ohhhh, yeah. I guess that makes more sense," agreed Red Robin.

Batman pressed a button on the computer. A video screen came to life with a recording of Silverback from earlier in the evening.

"We are the Animilitia!" the gorilla said.

Red Robin pummeled another robot that had crept up behind him. "Four animal-themed villains working together. Why? What's the angle?"

"It's not just them, Red Robin," said Batman, switching to another video screen that pulled up surveillance footage from S.T.A.R. Labs and Gotham National Bank. Images of the robotic tiger, wolf, and bat filled the screen.

"There are also these," said Batman.

"You always say there's a pattern," said Red Robin. "So what's the pattern?"

Batman pondered for a moment and then spoke a command to the Batcomputer: "Map all the robberies and break-ins committed by the Animilitia, including the five earlier ones by Cheetah and Croc."

Eight flashing dots appeared atop a map of Gotham City.

"Now include all reported crimes that were committed by robotic animals."

Three more flashing dots appeared.

Batman peered at the map and pointed to one building, "All eleven crime scenes form a circle around this spot."

"Aah! The Aviary," said Alfred, who had just entered the Batcave and was peering over Batman's shoulder. "It is Gotham City's newest and tallest building."

"It's also a massive feat of engineering," said Batman as he quickly looked up data on the building. "According to this news report, it was built by the only surviving member of a wealthy high-society family. Oswald Cobblepot invested his inheritance and seven years of his life to construct the Aviary."

"By the way, Bruce Wayne is expected to appear at the grand opening of the Aviary tonight," said Alfred. "Your tuxedo and invitation are ready for you upstairs. Try not to be late . . . as usual."

Bruce turned to glare at Alfred, but the butler was already walking up the stairs to exit the Batcave.

CHAPTER 7

Spotlights swept through the Gotham City skyline later that night as hundreds of limousines arrived outside the Aviary Building. Elite members of Gotham City's very highest society, dressed in tuxedos and luxurious evening gowns, entered the building and were whisked by elevator to the brightly lit penthouse. As they stepped into the room, several partygoers gasped at the breathtaking three-hundred-and-sixty-degree view of the city.

The party was already in full swing when a tuxedo-clad Bruce Wayne arrived, and he quickly walked over to James Gordon, the police commissioner of Gotham City.

Gordon was one of Batman's most trusted allies, but the police commissioner did not know that Bruce Wayne was secretly Batman. Tonight Gordon was dressed in a black tuxedo and white bow tie, quite different from his usual crumpled suit and long overcoat. The frown on his face made it clear that he was not enjoying the party.

"Good evening, Commissioner Gordon," said Bruce.

Gordon grimaced and said, "If you say so, Mr. Wayne. I hate these kinds of parties. I spend the entire time dodging old ladies who think I can fix the potholes on their streets."

Bruce smiled in sympathy and said, "Well, at least the building is impressive."

"I guess so," conceded Gordon. "But why build it? It might just be the cop in me, but I think that Cobblepot is up to something."

A voice called from the other side of the room, "Yoo-hoo! Oh, Bruce. Bruce Wayne? Over here, dear heart!"

It was Gladys Windsmere, the queen of Gotham City's high society. Waving her champagne glass in front of her to clear a path, she expertly made her way over to Bruce Wayne's side and clamped her hand over his arm.

"Oh, good evening, Ms. Windsmere," said Bruce, trapped in place as she held him tightly.

"Ms. Windsmere?" she said in a shocked voice. "How *could* you, Bruce? We're such close friends. More like a family, really. You *must* call me Gladys. I simply *insist*!"

"Of course . . . Gladys," he said, forcing a smile. "Have you met our host yet? I'd like to congratulate him. This place is really something."

Gladys wrinkled her nose as if she had smelled something foul.

"Oswald Cobblepot?" she said with disdain. "Horrible man. Nearly as rich as you, Bruce, but he is *quite* odd. I'll fetch him for you."

She then turned to notice Gordon and said, "Well, hello. I don't believe we've had the pleasure of meeting."

"How rude of me," said Bruce. "Gladys, this is Police Commissioner James Gordon."

"Oh, *really*?" said Gladys with great interest as she released her hand from Bruce's arm and grabbed Gordon's wrist. As she led Gordon away, she said, "You and I simply *must* chat, Commissioner. You see, there is this pothole in the middle of my block. . . ."

Gordon looked back at Bruce for help, but someone else was now standing next to Bruce. It was Oliver Queen, who was secretly Green Arrow. He knew that Bruce Wayne was Batman.

"Brucie baby! What's the good word?" Oliver said loudly as he grasped Bruce's hand.

"Oliver Queen," Bruce replied heartily. "Oh, you know me. Living the life, living the dream."

Queen then lowered his voice and whispered, "Anything new on our Furry Freak Friends?"

Bruce looked around to make sure no one overheard their conversation and replied, "Nothing yet. I'll let you know."

Just then, Gladys pushed her way through the crowd, escorting the host of the party.

"Here we are," she said, "Bruce Wayne . . . meet Oswald Cobblepot."

"It's a pleasure, Mr. Cobblepot," said Bruce.

"The pleasure is all yours," said Cobblepot as he extended his limp hand for a quick handshake with Bruce. "Do you appreciate my Aviary, Mr. Wayne? It's Gotham City's tallest building. Taller even than the Wayne Enterprises Tower, I'm afraid."

"It's impressive, to be sure," said Bruce. "I can see why you call it the Aviary. The views up here are breathtaking. You must feel like a bird all the way up here. I bet you're going to get a heck of a view of the Midas Heart asteroid when it passes by tomorrow night."

Cobblepot gave a sickly smile in response, but the mention of the asteroid seemed to make him agitated. Bruce observed that Cobblepot was making low clucking sounds, and his eyes were darting around the room. Cobblepot squeezed his right eye tightly around his monocle, which caused a digital microphone within the eyepiece to scan the room. While he glanced at Bruce Wayne and his companions, Cobblepot started listening to the conversation of two women who were standing on the other side of the room.

"Did you see him waddle?" asked one woman. "He's *so* disgusting!"

"Weird little penguin," said the other woman. "And that beak of his? Dreadful!"

"Mr. Cobblepot? Are you all right?" asked Bruce.

Something seemed to snap back in place for Cobblepot, and he smiled at his guests.

"I am indeed, my boy," he said. "I am better than all right. I am Oswald Cobblepot. And this will be a night to *remember*! If you'll excuse me, it's time for my speech."

With that, Cobblepot waddled to the front of the room and clambered up onto a stage. The lights dimmed, and a spotlight suddenly illuminated him. The room quieted so he could speak.

"Ladies and gentlemen of high society," Cobblepot called out. "Welcome to my little perch at the top of the Aviary. You were promised surprises tonight, and here they are. Gaze upon our ecological salvation, courtesy of my company, Bumbershoot Mechanics!"

Cobblepot turned around to point dramatically as a large platform slowly rose behind him. Atop the platform were the robotic wolf, tiger, and bat. All three robots moved in unison, stretching their shiny metallic limbs to grow even larger.

Bruce Wayne and Oliver Queen looked on in astonishment.

CHAPTER 8

The stunned crowd murmured at the sight of the three mechanical animals as Cobblepot continued to speak.

"Bumbershoot Mechanics proudly presents these three unmanned robots," he said. "They are designed to right the wrongs that mankind has heaped upon our environment. Together we can steer this planet to live harmoniously with nature again. When humanity's greed poisons the earth, Bumbershoot Mechanics will be there with solutions!"

A large screen descended from the ceiling and showed video footage of the three Cyber Animals in action. The wolf used its metallic armor to clear a cave-in at a coal mine. The tiger stopped an unmanned oil well that was burning in the middle of the desert. The Cyber Bat fired lasers at poachers on a whaling ship that were attempting to harpoon a giant sperm whale.

With a proud smile, Cobblepot continued, "When our systems break down, doing more harm than good, we will be there to lend a hand. When unimaginable cruelty becomes the harsh reality of commerce, we will be there to help. Bumbershoot Mechanics' Cyber Animals are inspired by Mother Nature's perfect designs and charged with the preservation and restoration of the natural world!"

As the crowd applauded, Cobblepot basked in the attention. In the back of the room Oliver Queen turned to Bruce Wayne and said, "Those look just like the same—"

"They *are* the same," interrupted Bruce, who then discreetly adjusted the mini-camera located in his tie and whispered into his communicator device, "Are you seeing this, Red Robin?"

Back in the Batcave, Red Robin was eating a bowl of cereal while watching a live feed of the party from Bruce's camera.

"Oh yeah, I've got it," he replied.

"Pull everything you can find on Bumbershoot Mechanics," Bruce instructed.

Red Robin quickly started punching keys on the Batcomputer.

"On it! Bring me home a couple of pigs in a blanket, some sliders, and a handful of crab puffs, won't you?" said Red Robin, but there was silence. "Hello? Bruce? Yeah, guess that's a no."

In the Aviary penthouse the Cyber Animals had been removed, and another man had joined Cobblepot on the stage.

"Allow me to present to you my genius, the zoologist who engineered these amazing creatures: Dr. Kirk Langstrom!" said Cobblepot.

Langstrom nervously wiped his brow, cleared his throat several times, and shakily addressed the crowd.

"Um, thank you," he said, his voice barely above a whisper. "Animals. Nature designed them to fit harmoniously into their environment. Every aspect of their existence serves a purpose. Which is most assuredly *not* something that happens with people . . ."

Langstrom paused and then continued, "Uh, that was a joke. Well, okay. So, what if robotic engineering stood on the shoulders of nature's perfect design? Well, we might be able to make cyber organisms that could help extend the reach of humanity. We might be able to create a mechanical tool that would empower us, one that could inspire us to dream even bigger."

Langstrom grew more excited, and his voice rose as he continued, "Man has strong animal instincts, and these cybers will help explore and control those instincts!"

As the crowd applauded, Bruce whispered to Oliver, "Langstrom will know what Cobblepot is planning. We need to talk to him."

"There's no way Cobblepot will let anyone get close to him tonight."

"Not here," Bruce lowered his voice even further. "Not dressed like this."

"Got it," said Oliver. "So how do we keep tabs on him?"

Bruce reached into his tuxedo pocket and removed a tiny gadget. Two bat-shaped wings flicked out of it.

"We can use this tracking device," he said. "I just need to get close enough to slip it on him."

"No, you don't," said Oliver with a grin. "Give it here."

Bruce frowned as he handed the tracker to Oliver, saying, "Be careful with that. It's—"

Before Bruce could finish his sentence, Oliver had

lined up his shot, flicked the tracker from his hand, and sent it sailing across the room. The tracker was soon nestled in Langstrom's pants cuff.

"Bull's-eye!" boasted Oliver.

"Nice shot," said Bruce.

Onstage, Langstrom was still speaking, although he seemed nervous again and spoke with less confidence.

"Who knows?" he said, pausing to wipe his brow. "Perhaps these cybers can even help us tame the animals inside of us all."

Suddenly, Cobblepot wheeled around to glare at Langstrom. With a shove, he pushed Langstrom out of the spotlight.

"That's enough. Shoo! Shoo!" he said angrily, elbowing Langstrom off the stage.

The puzzled crowd offered polite applause, and Cobblepot struggled to regain his composure. Looking down into the crowd, he activated his electronic monocle again to eavesdrop on a discussion between Gladys Windsmere and another woman.

"Oh, my dear," said Gladys. "Can you imagine Cobblepot at the club with us? I don't care *how* many robot friends he builds!"

"I'm surprised he didn't build an ugly little penguin

that would look just like him!" said the other woman with a laugh.

Cobblepot's face darkened, and he slammed the tip of his umbrella on the stage.

"This evening is at an *end*!" he shouted. "I bid you all good night!"

The guests reacted with confusion, unsure whether Cobblepot was serious.

"I said good *night*!" he screamed, and then touched a button on his umbrella. The robotic animals jumped onto the stage and stood beside him. Each animal let out a menacing growl and started advancing toward the crowd. In a panic, the room quickly emptied as the frightened partygoers ran to the elevators.

As Oliver Queen watched the guests depart, he turned to Bruce Wayne and said, "Quite a party, wasn't it?"

But Bruce was already gone. He was rushing back to the Batcave.

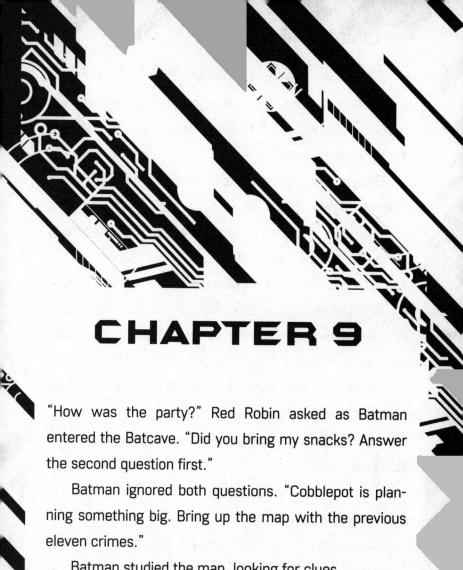

CHAPTER 9

"How was the party?" Red Robin asked as Batman entered the Batcave. "Did you bring my snacks? Answer the second question first."

Batman ignored both questions. "Cobblepot is planning something big. Bring up the map with the previous eleven crimes."

Batman studied the map, looking for clues.

"All eleven crime scenes are equal distances from each other and from the Aviary Building. All but these two," said Batman, pointing to two locations just east of the Aviary.

"Those two?" asked Red Robin. "But why?"

Batman thought for a moment and then declared, "Because there's a crime scene missing . . . one that hasn't happened yet."

Batman pointed to a spot on the map and said, "Here—at the Gotham City Zoo."

Red Robin's fingers flew on the computer keyboard, pulling up the zoo's Web site.

"The zoo has a pair of rare California condors on display through tomorrow only," he said.

Batman was already pulling on his cowl and jumping into the cockpit of the Batmobile.

"Alert the others to meet us at the zoo," he said as he revved the engine.

Red Robin jumped out of his seat and ran to the Batcycle.

As Batman and Red Robin raced to the zoo, they sped past the Aviary Building, where the penthouse was still brightly lit. The party was over, but a new group now filled the room. Oswald Cobblepot paced back and forth, muttering to himself angrily. The four members of the Animilitia were also present, but they were ignoring Cobblepot. Cheetah reclined on a couch, lapping milk out of a champagne glass. Killer Croc was leaning over a table and using his giant hand to shovel shrimp and caviar into his open mouth. Man-Bat seemed to be asleep, hanging upside down from a chandelier. And Silverback was drinking water from a fishbowl, even swallowing a few of the fish.

"Those insipid morons dare to treat *me* like a freak? An outcast? An animal?" Cobblepot said, raising his voice. "They dare to call me Penguin, do they? Well, Gotham City will see the errors of its ways. If they treat me like an animal, then I will *act* like an animal. They'll rue the day they ever called Oswald Cobblepot the Penguin!"

Cobblepot banged his umbrella on a table, causing the four villains to look up in surprise.

"We are the apex predators of Gotham City," Cobblepot screamed. "And we will bring this city to its *knees*!"

The four members of the Animilitia exchanged looks, not sure how to react to Cobblepot's outburst. Then Silverback smiled and softly intoned, "Penguin! Penguin! Penguin!"

Soon Cheetah and Killer Croc joined in, "Pen-guin! Pen-guin! Pen-guin!" they chanted together.

Cobblepot took a deep bow and said, "Yes, I am one of you now. I've embraced the animal in me! Soon, all of

Gotham will know that I *am* the Penguin!

He faced the villains and continued, "You have one remaining assignment. Finish the last job, and I will see to it that *all* of Gotham City bows to us."

The Animilitia burst into applause. Killer Croc jumped to his feet, knocking over the table. Cheetah scratched at the air. Silverback thumped his paws on his furry chest. Above them all, Man-Bat stretched his wings and let out a loud screech.

The Penguin smiled. Nothing could stop him now.

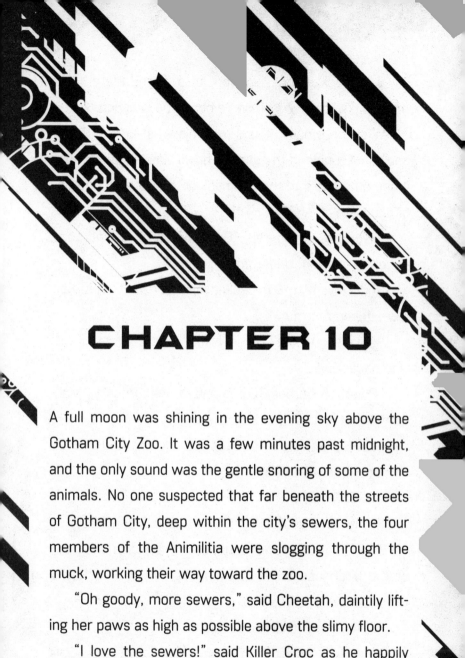

CHAPTER 10

A full moon was shining in the evening sky above the Gotham City Zoo. It was a few minutes past midnight, and the only sound was the gentle snoring of some of the animals. No one suspected that far beneath the streets of Gotham City, deep within the city's sewers, the four members of the Animilitia were slogging through the muck, working their way toward the zoo.

"Oh goody, more sewers," said Cheetah, daintily lifting her paws as high as possible above the slimy floor.

"I love the sewers!" said Killer Croc as he happily sloshed through the sewage.

Silverback stopped in front of a rusted metal grate that blocked their way. "We're here," he whispered.

With three quick blasts from his wrist lasers, Silverback shot a hole in the grate. The villains leaped through it and emerged into the darkness of the Gotham City Zoo birdhouse.

Silverback whispered, "Grab the condors, and complete the mission. Understood?"

Suddenly, Man-Bat cocked his head and emitted a low-pitched murmur.

"What's he doing?" Croc asked, eager to get the mission underway.

"Quiet!" Silverback commanded. He turned to Man-Bat. "What is it? What do you hear?"

Man-Bat shivered. His eyes grew wider. And then he let out with a piercing scream.

SKREEEEEECH!

"About time you guys got here," said Green Arrow.

The Animilitia spun around. Standing at the other end of the birdhouse were Batman, Nightwing, Red Robin, Green Arrow, and The Flash.

"Take them!" ordered Batman.

Silverback turned to his companions and said, "Split up and complete the mission!"

The giant ape extended his wrists, firing lasers at the heroes. The Flash zoomed over to Silverback, running around him and trying to land a punch. But while he was focused on Silverback, the other villains ran in different directions.

CHAPTER 11

"I'll handle Cheetah," Batman called out, brandishing his grappling hook.

"Dibs on the ape," yelled The Flash. "He's over there, heading to the gorilla enclosure."

"Careful," cautioned Green Arrow. "Silverback is—"

Before he could finish his sentence, The Flash had zoomed past him in pursuit of the villain.

CRASH!

Killer Croc had just punched his way through the doors of the reptile house.

"That's my cue," called out Green Arrow as he ran after Croc.

Nightwing turned to Red Robin and said, "Come on. I think I know where Man-Bat flew off to."

As the heroes ran through the zoo, Batman stealthily crawled up the exterior of the big-cat house. He then hopped over the wall and landed within the lush, jungle-like habitat. It was dark inside, and Batman could only see the yellow eyes of the exhibit's felines staring at him. A few low growls rumbled from the big cats. Suddenly, the voice of Cheetah taunted him in the darkness.

"How's your night vision, Batman?" she asked. "We cats can see in the dark, you know."

Batman quickly activated the night vision in his cowl and saw dozens of man-eating cats perched in trees all around him, glaring at him and growling. But there was no sign of Cheetah. Then he heard her voice again, this time coming from the trees above him.

"You dress as one of us, but secretly you fear your animal nature," Cheetah said. "You bury your animal instincts beneath layers of duty and order. Allow me to *carve* it out for you!"

Cheetah jumped down from the leafy branch of a tree, her claws extended. She lashed out at Batman as he raised his arms in defense. Cheetah's talons caught the metal gauntlets on his gloves, and sparks flew as her razor-sharp claws scraped against the metal.

OOOF!

With a crash, Batman collided with a branch of a tree and toppled to the ground. Behind him, several panthers were eyeing him angrily, and in front, Cheetah was looking down as though at her prey. Batman quickly got to his feet and jumped onto an adjacent tree branch for cover.

"Did you forget that cats love to climb trees, Batman?" she asked with a laugh.

Batman reached into his Utility Belt and extracted an explosive Batarang.

"Your trinkets won't help you," Cheetah called out as she caught the Batarang midair.

BLAM!

The Batarang exploded with a flash of white light. Cheetah was knocked off-balance and tumbled backward to the ground. One villain down—three to go.

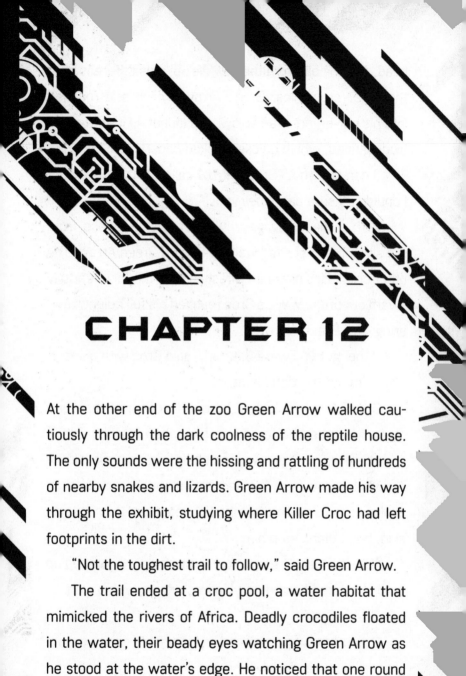

CHAPTER 12

At the other end of the zoo Green Arrow walked cautiously through the dark coolness of the reptile house. The only sounds were the hissing and rattling of hundreds of nearby snakes and lizards. Green Arrow made his way through the exhibit, studying where Killer Croc had left footprints in the dirt.

"Not the toughest trail to follow," said Green Arrow.

The trail ended at a croc pool, a water habitat that mimicked the rivers of Africa. Deadly crocodiles floated in the water, their beady eyes watching Green Arrow as he stood at the water's edge. He noticed that one round head, only visible from the nostrils up, was different from the other crocodiles. Green Arrow smiled and reached into his quiver, drew an arrow, and launched it at the protruding head, which quickly ducked underwater.

"I can see you," Green Arrow called out. "And even if I couldn't, I sure can *smell* you!"

With a menacing grin, Killer Croc slowly rose from the swamp and started walking toward Green Arrow. The other crocodiles near him thrashed their tails and fearfully swam out of the way as Croc reached his full height, towering over Green Arrow.

"I thought you were Batman," said Croc with a sneer. "*You*, I'm not worried about."

Green Arrow quickly fired one arrow, and then two more. All three shattered into bits when they hit Croc's rock-hard skin. Croc was reaching out to grab Green Arrow, but the hero jumped out of reach and fired an explosive arrow. The bomb detonated on Croc's scaly skin, but it didn't stop him.

"Uh-oh!" said Green Arrow with a gulp. He jumped up onto a covered balcony, trying to come up with a plan.

SNAP! SNAP!

Green Arrow spun around just in time to see two giant crocodiles, their massive mouths snapping open and shut as they moved toward the hero. Green Arrow turned again and collided with Killer Croc.

Green Arrow quickly loaded three net arrows and fired. Two arrows covered the crocodiles in nets, and the middle arrow wrapped a net around Killer Croc.

Croc ripped the net apart with ease.

Killer Croc grabbed Green Arrow and threw him to the ground. The villain then wrapped the torn netting around Green Arrow, pinning his arms to his sides.

"Let's see you shoot now! Ha-ha-ha!" Croc said as he walked away.

Green Arrow couldn't move his arms, but he was able to roll to his side. He strained to stretch his neck toward his quiver and with great effort managed to extract an arrow with his teeth. He then rolled over to his other side and carefully nocked the arrow to his bowstring. He balanced the bow between his feet, holding the arrow with his teeth.

"Hey, Croc!" he called out.

Killer Croc spun around just as the arrow flew right into his open mouth. The villain chomped down hard on the arrow, breaking the shaft.

KER-BLAM!

The arrowhead exploded inside Croc's mouth. Green

knockout gas slowly seeped out of his nostrils and mouth. The enraged villain lumbered toward Green Arrow, his giant arms extended. Then Croc's eyes crossed, and Killer Croc fell to the ground, snoring.

"Phew," said Green Arrow as he quickly freed himself from the netting.

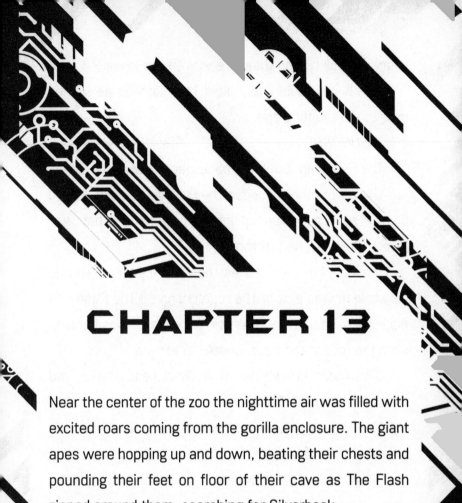

CHAPTER 13

Near the center of the zoo the nighttime air was filled with excited roars coming from the gorilla enclosure. The giant apes were hopping up and down, beating their chests and pounding their feet on floor of their cave as The Flash zipped around them, searching for Silverback.

"Come on out, Silverback," The Flash called. "You know I'll find you."

Silverback slowly emerged from a dark corner of the cave, smiling as he stepped into the light.

"I don't need to hide from you, speedster," he said as he thumped his chest with a giant paw. "I've calculated every possibility, and they all end with you losing!"

"We'll see about that," said The Flash as he rushed over to the taunting ape.

WHOOOSH!

The Flash ran, but Silverback leaped out of the way!

"Hey, what the—" began The Flash as he spun around on the spot and stepped into a coiled rope that was located beneath his left foot.

"Aaack!" he cried out as the rope tightened around his ankle. It was a trap! The rope ensnared The Flash and flipped him upside down. Within seconds he was hanging from the roof of the cave, unable to escape.

Silverback jumped down from a nearby tree and walked over to The Flash.

"I would say you were a worthy opponent," the ape gloated, "but I hate to lie."

"That's it!" yelled The Flash as he thrashed his arms in the air, trying to hit Silverback. With a laugh, the giant ape clambered out of the gorilla enclosure. The Flash continued to twist in the air, trying to wriggle out of the ropes without success.

Just then, four gorillas approached The Flash and stared curiously at the upside-down and struggling hero.

"Oh, hey there, big guys," The Flash said nervously. "I

should be out of your fur in just a—"

Before he could finish his sentence, one gorilla poked The Flash's chest with its giant finger. The hero swayed in the air.

"Hey, don't do that! Scram!" yelled The Flash as another gorilla smacked him, sending the hero swinging in the other direction.

The gorillas smiled at each other and gathered closer, each reaching out a paw to keep The Flash swinging high above their heads.

The Flash groaned and said, "This is embarrassing. I'm the Fastest Man Alive! I can't get beaten by a length of rope!"

Suddenly, a thought popped into his mind, and he said, "Wait, it's just a length of rope!"

As he swung through the air, The Flash wiggled his foot. The rope was bound tightly around his left ankle, but he was still able to move his right foot. He moved his right foot faster and faster. The gorillas watched in fascination as The Flash's foot became a red blur, rubbing against the rope. Soon, the rope started to smoke. The Flash rubbed his foot as fast as possible. The rope caught fire from the friction and snapped. With a thud, The Flash fell to the ground.

"Sorry to break up the party, fellas, but I've gotta run!" The Flash said to the disappointed gorillas as he zoomed out of the cave and quickly caught up to Silverback.

"Impossible! I calculated zero means of escape," said the astonished ape as he lifted an arm and fired his wrist laser at The Flash.

The Flash avoided the laser blasts and darted around Silverback.

"You like playing games?" The Flash asked. "Here's one for you."

In an instant The Flash had circled around Silverback so many times that the giant ape was surrounded by a dozen afterimages of the speeding hero. Silverback spun in circles, tossing punches through the air.

"Try to pick the real one before I knock you out," called out The Flash as he ran faster and faster around the giant ape.

Silverback's cyber eye began clicking. He was running mathematical calculations as quickly as possible, trying to analyze The Flash's movements, but the hero was moving too fast for Silverback's internal computer. The dozen images of The Flash all began landing punches. One final punch connected with Silverback's jaw, and the giant ape fell to the ground, knocked unconscious.

From their nearby cave, the gorillas had been watching the fight with interest. One gorilla started clapping his hands, and soon all of the other gorillas were applauding.

The Flash looked over at them, took a deep bow, and called out, "Thanks, guys. Thanks very much!"

CHAPTER 14

Red Robin and Nightwing stood inside the zoo's bat cavern exhibit, shining their flashlights into the darkness.

"This place gives me the creeps," Red Robin said.

"What's the big deal?" asked Nightwing. "Aren't you based in a cave?"

"Yeah," said Red Robin, "but that cave has computers and lights and stuff."

Nightwing shined his light up a tunnel. Hanging from the ceiling was Man-Bat, his wings tightly wrapped around his eyes.

"There he is!" Red Robin said with excitement.

"Shhh!" Nightwing said. "You stay here. I'm going to approach him quietly."

As Nightwing crept along the edge of the tunnel, Red Robin decided that he had a better plan. He reached into his Utility Belt and removed a throwing disk. With a flick of his wrist, Red Robin flung it at Man-Bat's head.

SCREEEEECH!

Man-Bat let out an enraged cry and started flapping his leathery wings. Soon, the tunnel was filled with thousands of bats, all screaming and swooping around Nightwing and Red Robin.

"Behind you!" shouted Nightwing as Man-Bat swooped toward his friend.

The angry beast extended its sharp talons and sunk them into Red Robin's leg. Within seconds Man-Bat was flying out of the cavern, carrying the struggling Red Robin in his claws.

Nightwing frantically raced after them, saying to himself, "Oh man. Batman is going to *kill* me!"

Fortunately, Man-Bat didn't travel far with his victim. The creature hovered high above the zoo, watching with interest as Batman used handcuffs to secure Cheetah, Killer Croc, and Silverback to the fountain at the center of the zoo. The Flash and Green Arrow looked on in approval.

"Nice work," said Batman to the other heroes. "They didn't give you much trouble, did they?"

The Flash and Green Arrow both exchanged embarrassed glances.

"Are you kidding?" said Green Arrow with a smile.

"Not even a little," added The Flash, still a little dizzy from his session as a punching bag for the gorillas.

Killer Croc thrashed at the tight bonds and muttered to Silverback, "I thought this plan was foolproof!"

"Correct," whispered Silverback as he looked up. "I've requested backup."

Just then, Man-Bat swooped above them. The creature was still carrying Red Robin.

"Don't worry! I've got this!" shouted Nightwing as he ran after them. Nightwing electrified one of his batons and threw it. It collided with Man-Bat, who opened his talons. Red Robin tumbled through the air and landed with a giant splash in the middle of the flamingo pond.

"We're over here!" Cheetah shouted to Man-Bat, who was still circling the zoo. "Free us!" Man-Bat dived toward them.

"Don't let him untie them," yelled Batman.

"He's fast," said Green Arrow as he launched arrow after arrow at Man-Bat.

"And I'm faster!" boasted The Flash as he ran toward the creature.

Just as The Flash was about to grab Man-Bat, the creature opened its mouth and spat a sticky green substance on the ground. The Flash skidded into the gooey liquid and was instantly trapped in place.

"Gross!" yelled The Flash as he struggled to lift his feet.

Man-Bat spread its wings and swooped down to the three villains. Batman tried to land a punch, but the creature threw him into the trees.

With a flick of his talons, Man-Bat cut through the handcuffs handily. The Animilitia were free again. They stood together and faced the heroes.

Silverback's cyber eye clicked as he smiled and said, "Reinforcements will arrive in three, two, one—"

BLAM!

The robotic wolf, tiger, and bat sailed over the gates of the zoo and landed with a thud next to the heroes. The wolf and tiger both snapped their powerful jaws. The mechanical eyes of the Cyber Bat glowed red as it prepared to fire deadly lasers.

"Great," muttered Green Arrow. "These guys again."

"Dismantle the heroes!" commanded Silverback. Then Man-Bat and the Cyber Bat soared into the air.

Silverback and Cheetah each reached up to grab the Cyber Bat. Killer Croc wrapped his giant hand around Man-Bat's extended claws. Within seconds the Animilitia disappeared into the skies, with the sound of Silverback's harsh laugh echoing above the zoo.

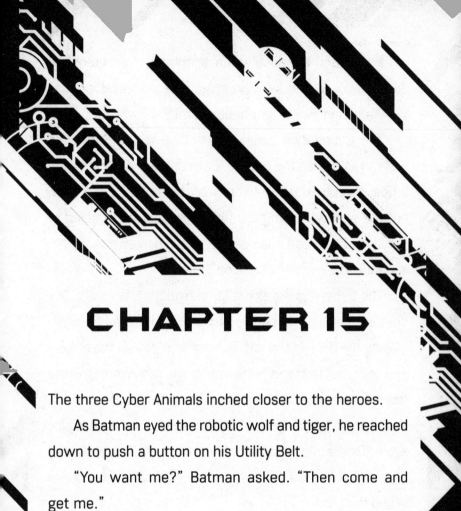

CHAPTER 15

The three Cyber Animals inched closer to the heroes.

As Batman eyed the robotic wolf and tiger, he reached down to push a button on his Utility Belt.

"You want me?" Batman asked. "Then come and get me."

ZOOM!

With a mighty roar the Batmobile crashed through the zoo's gates. Batman touched the button again, and the car skidded to a stop and opened its canopy. Batman jumped over the side of the Batmobile and expertly landed in the driver's seat.

He pushed the accelerator to the floor and launched out of the zoo and into the streets of Gotham City. The wolf and tiger were right behind him!

The Cyber Wolf quickly caught up to the Batmobile and ran alongside the vehicle. Batman turned the steering wheel sharply left; the tiger was able to make the turn, but the wolf was going too fast. The creature tumbled to the side of the road and collided with a parked car. Within seconds the wolf was back on its feet.

The Cyber Tiger was not far behind the Batmobile. The creature poured on speed and launched itself into the air, nipping the back of the car. Batman abruptly hit the brakes and spun, but didn't hit either robot. The radar screen in the Batmobile started blinking—the Cyber Bat had returned. It was flying toward him, so Batman floored the accelerator again. The Batmobile sped away with a roar. Sirens started screaming as Gotham City police cars and hovercrafts joined the chase.

VROOOOM!

Two other heroes had arrived on the Batcycle. Red Robin expertly steered, while his passenger Green Arrow launched arrows at the Cyber Bat.

"Top priority is their air support," Batman commanded.

"I can help with that," Green Arrow said. An explosive

arrow connected with the robotic bat, causing the creature to falter momentarily. But the bat quickly recovered and turned its head in the direction of the Batcycle. Red lasers surged from its eyes. Red Robin swerved the bike, but it skidded out of control.

"Jump!" yelled Red Robin.

Green Arrow quickly fired a grapple arrow, which lodged itself into a nearby building. Just as the Batcycle was hit by an explosive laser blast, Green Arrow grabbed Red Robin. The two heroes soared through the air for a few moments and then touched down on top of a police hovercraft.

"What the heck?" yelled a startled policeman from inside the vehicle.

"Thanks, officer," said Green Arrow as he climbed into the craft. "This is why I love cops. Follow that bat!"

The hovercraft zoomed off in pursuit of the Cyber Bat.

BLAM!

An explosive arrow slammed into the robotic bat, causing it to topple in the air. The Cyber Bat's head slowly rotated to face the police hovercraft. The creature's eyes fired a red laser blast, knocking out the hovercraft's motor. The disabled craft started losing altitude.

"Take care of the officer. This is my stop!" yelled Green Arrow, leaping from the hood.

"Sure thing," said Red Robin as he wrapped his arm around the policeman and jumped out of the craft. Together they sailed through the air and crashed through the window of a nearby office building just seconds before the hovercraft crashed to the ground.

Green Arrow had managed to land on top of the speeding Batmobile and was frantically firing arrows at the mechanical bat. The Cyber Bat was moving closer, its red eyes glowing.

Green Arrow lost sight of the bat as they drove through a tunnel, but he reached into his quiver and withdrew an electronic arrow.

Atop the vehicle Green Arrow took careful aim. Just as the Batmobile zoomed out of the tunnel, Green Arrow shot his arrow into the Cyber Bat's head. The bat slammed into the middle of the video screen that was broadcasting news of the Midas Heart asteroid.

KER-BLAM!

A huge shower of electrical sparks cascaded out of the video screen. The Cyber Bat swayed in the air, its internal circuits fried by the giant blast of electricity. It crashed to the ground, a thick stream of black smoke emerging from within its mechanical body.

"Collect that robot," instructed Batman. "I'm going to need to run some tests."

"Roger that," replied Green Arrow as he jumped off the moving car.

The voice of Nightwing came over the Batmobile's communicator link.

"Heads-up, you've got construction on Twenty-Third Street," said Nightwing.

"Perfect," said Batman. "Meet me there."

The robotic wolf and tiger were racing alongside the Batmobile, frantically snapping their metal jaws and trying to grab on to the vehicle.

Batman flipped a switch on the dashboard and launched the Batmobile into turbo overdrive. A construction site was just ahead, and the Batmobile fired a laser blast into the air. The laser hit a giant steel girder that was hanging from a construction crane. The girder was knocked loose and plummeted toward the ground.

Batman expertly swerved the Batmobile to the left. The tiger quickly changed course and followed Batman. The wolf was not so quick, though.

CLANG!

The steel girder fell with a crash on top of the wolf,

temporarily trapping the creature. Just as the wolf was about to free itself, Nightwing threw an electrical baton directly at the wolf's head. The impact short-circuited the creature's wiring. The wolf stopped moving, its scorched robotic body covered in black scars.

"That's two," said Nightwing into his communicator.

The Batmobile roared through the streets of Gotham City. The Cyber Tiger was running alongside the vehicle, hungrily snapping its jaws next to Batman. No matter how fast Batman accelerated the Batmobile, the tiger was just as fast.

ZOOM!

Just then, The Flash appeared on the other side of the Batmobile.

"Sorry, sorry," The Flash said. "It took forever to get my boots unstuck from that Man-Bat goo."

The Flash then zoomed over to the other side of the Batmobile and ran alongside the Cyber Tiger. The Flash reached over and knocked on the tiger's metallic head.

"You want to race?" The Flash asked. "Because I can race."

The tiger snarled and opened its jaws, trying to snap off The Flash's hand.

The Batmobile peeled down a side street, but the

tiger continued to chase The Flash. As the hero ran even faster, so did the tiger.

"I'm impressed," said The Flash. "But I still think I can do something you can't—"

Before he could finish his sentence, The Flash skidded to a halt just in front of a concrete wall.

"I can *stop*," he said.

The Cyber Tiger's eyes widened as it approached the wall. The creature frantically flexed its paws, trying to stop.

BLAM!

The tiger crashed into the wall. Sparks filled the air as the robot's internal circuits overloaded. The creature shuddered briefly and then toppled to the ground.

"And that's three," said The Flash into his communicator.

"I'll want to examine all three robots in the cave," was the response from Batman as he turned the Batmobile around and headed toward Wayne Manor. The four members of the Animilitia were still at large. This long night was not over yet.

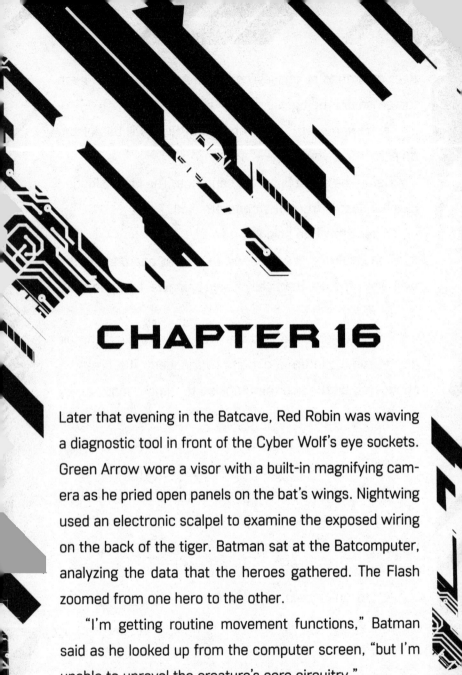

CHAPTER 16

Later that evening in the Batcave, Red Robin was waving a diagnostic tool in front of the Cyber Wolf's eye sockets. Green Arrow wore a visor with a built-in magnifying camera as he pried open panels on the bat's wings. Nightwing used an electronic scalpel to examine the exposed wiring on the back of the tiger. Batman sat at the Batcomputer, analyzing the data that the heroes gathered. The Flash zoomed from one hero to the other.

"I'm getting routine movement functions," Batman said as he looked up from the computer screen, "but I'm unable to unravel the creature's core circuitry."

"I can try to reroute it," Red Robin offered, "but this is some next-level engineering."

Nightwing agreed. "These things are built to be tough *and* fast. Dr. Langstrom is a genius."

Green Arrow pulled out some wires from the Cyber Bat. "Wiring is mostly copper—"

"Which explains why Croc was at the copper quarry," Batman finished.

"You guys want me to take a look at anything?" The Flash asked as he zipped around the lab. "Can I help? Huh? Can I?"

"Why don't you take a seat, motormouth?" said Nightwing with annoyance. "The adults are working."

The Flash frowned and threw himself onto a chair, pouting.

Batman scrolled through articles on Oswald Cobblepot. "What are you playing at, Cobblepot?" he asked the screen. "Something's not right. These robberies, in the last three, the—"

"Furry Four?" interrupted The Flash.

"Good one," said Green Arrow with a laugh. "I was going to call them the Flea Circus!"

Batman ignored them and continued, "As I was saying, in the last three robberies, the Animilitia left behind what they *supposedly* broke in for."

Batman brought up videos of the robberies at the zoo, the bank, and the jewelry store.

"They didn't steal anything because we *stopped* them," said Green Arrow proudly.

"No," said Batman. "It was because they weren't there to take anything. The robberies were just meant to distract us. The Animilitia went to these locations to *leave* something. But what?"

Batman opened a new window on the screen. "We'll never hack these robots without the man who created them. We need Langstrom."

"But how do we find him?" asked Red Robin.

Batman flicked a switch on the computer, and a red dot appeared atop a map of Gotham City.

BEEP! BEEP! BEEP!

"That's how," said Batman. "We'll use the tracker device that Green Arrow placed on Langstrom."

Nightwing studied the map and said, "It looks like the Animilitia has him at Cobblepot's company, Bumbershoot Mechanics."

"Let's go," said Batman as he pulled the cowl over his face. "Red Robin, I need you to continue to try to hack these robots; we need to know what Cobblepot is planning. Nightwing and Arrow, you come with me."

"What about me?" asked The Flash with dismay.

"I need you to check out every robbery location. See if you can find what they left behind. Do it fast."

"That's my middle name!" said The Flash. "Well, it's not *really* my middle name. My actual middle name is . . ."

The Flash looked around. The other heroes were already gone.

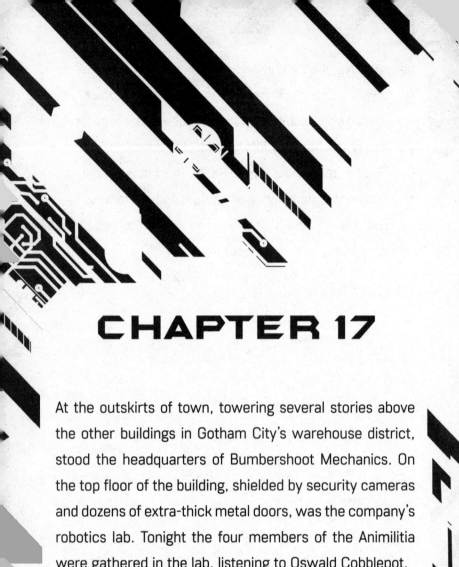

CHAPTER 17

At the outskirts of town, towering several stories above the other buildings in Gotham City's warehouse district, stood the headquarters of Bumbershoot Mechanics. On the top floor of the building, shielded by security cameras and dozens of extra-thick metal doors, was the company's robotics lab. Tonight the four members of the Animilitia were gathered in the lab, listening to Oswald Cobblepot.

"Is our last receiver in place at the zoo?" he demanded.

"Affirmative, Penguin," said Silverback.

"It went down just like you said it would, boss," added Killer Croc. "Nobody suspects a thing."

Cobblepot smiled and said, "Excellent news, my animal allies. The Midas Heart asteroid passes in less than twenty hours. That's when we will strike."

Atop the Bumbershoot Mechanics building, Batman and Nightwing landed softly on the roof. Batman removed the GPS tracking device from his Utility Belt.

"We'll sneak in, free Langstrom, and get out," he said, and then spoke into his communicator link, "Okay, Arrow. Now!"

Atop an adjoining building, Green Arrow nodded, drew back an arrow, and shot it directly at the window of the lab. The arrow crashed through the glass, soared through the air, and pierced the Penguin's top hat.

"Waaauk!" squawked the Penguin angrily. "That was my favorite hat!"

Cheetah ran to the window and reported, "It's the archer!"

The Penguin waddled over to the window and extended his umbrella through the broken glass. With the press of a button, the Penguin's umbrella became a blaster. He opened fire on Green Arrow, who ducked to avoid the laser blasts. The hero then jumped up and fired back, his arrow catching the Penguin's jacket collar and slamming him backward until he was pinned to the wall.

"End him!" screamed the Penguin furiously.

Cheetah and Silverback jumped through the broken window and landed on the rooftop near Green Arrow. The hero quickly shot two explosive arrows, giving him time to run to the edge of the building.

When he looked up, he saw that the explosive arrows had hit Silverback pretty hard. The ape's fur had been burned and peeled back to reveal hard, shiny metal—Silverback wasn't just a *bionic* ape. He was a *robotic* ape. But this piece of news would have to wait for later.

Green Arrow whispered into his communicator, "Okay, Batman. Two of them are after me, just like you said."

Batman checked the tracker again and said, "Okay, Langstrom should be directly below us."

Batman let fly an explosive Batarang.

BLAM!

The Batarang blasted a hole in the roof. Nightwing and Batman quickly jumped through the hole and dropped down on top of Man-Bat. The frightened creature started screaming and frantically flapping its wings, trying to loosen Batman's grip. One of Man-Bat's powerful wings tossed Nightwing across the room.

Killer Croc and the Penguin looked on in astonishment.

"Stop him!" ordered the Penguin.

Man-Bat took a running leap, with Batman still holding tight, and together they soared straight through the broken window. Man-Bat was frantically spinning and twisting, trying to dislodge his unwelcome passenger.

Inside the laboratory Nightwing slowly staggered to his feet. Suddenly, Killer Croc clamped one giant hand on Nightwing's shoulder and pulled back to deliver a powerhouse punch. Nightwing deftly ducked and then cartwheeled backward, causing Croc's fist to smash one of the lab's workbenches. Metallic robot pieces scattered across the floor.

Croc was throwing wild punches at Nightwing, who continued to jump up, down, and just beyond the reach of his opponent.

"If you want anything done right, you have to do it yourself," muttered the Penguin as he snuck up behind Nightwing and then poked the young hero with the tip of his umbrella.

ZZZZZAP!

An electric shock sent Nightwing crashing to the floor.

"Get rid of him!" ordered the Penguin.

"With pleasure, Mr. Penguin," replied Killer Croc as he roughly lifted Nightwing in his arms and tossed him out the window.

High above Bumbershoot Mechanics, Batman was still riding the frantically bucking Man-Bat and saw Nightwing come sailing through the window.

Batman spoke into his communicator link.

"Flash," he said, "incoming!"

"On it," replied The Flash as he zoomed to the street outside Bumbershoot Mechanics and then launched himself into the air. Seconds later he ran up the wall of the building and caught Nightwing in his open arms.

"I can't believe you saved me," Nightwing said groggily, still recovering from the Penguin's electrical shock.

"I know, me too," said The Flash. "I've never run up a building before. I'm kinda surprised it worked!"

"Wait, *what*?!" said Nightwing, now wide awake.

"All in a night's work," said The Flash as he dropped Nightwing onto the ground.

Above them Batman grappled to control Man-Bat. As the creature shrieked and kicked its legs, Batman suddenly noticed something that was attached to Man-Bat's pants. It was the tracking device!

"Langstrom?" asked Batman hesitantly.

Man-Bat quickly turned his head to stare at Batman. Was it possible, Batman wondered, that this really *was* Langstrom?

Thinking fast, Batman reached into his Utility Belt and extracted a sonic Batarang. He then activated it right next to Man-Bat's extra-sensitive ear, scrambling the creature's sonar.

SCREEEEECH!

Man-Bat cried out in pain, and soon the two were plummeting toward the street.

"Just relax, this won't hurt," Batman said as he removed a hypodermic needle from his Utility Belt and administered a sleeping serum to Man-Bat. As the creature drifted into a deep slumber, Batman extended his cape's glider wings and descended safely to the street. Green Arrow, The Flash, and Nightwing were waiting for them.

"The bad guys got away," The Flash said.

"Not all of them," said Batman as he gently placed Man-Bat on the ground. "Let's get him to the Batcave."

"Gee, great," said The Flash doubtfully. "We got the only bad guy who doesn't talk. What is *he* going to be able to tell us?"

CHAPTER 18

Back at the Batcave, Man-Bat was thrashing inside a thick Plexiglas cell, frantically pounding his fists on the walls. Batman was working at the Batcomputer, analyzing a blood sample, while the other heroes stared at the captive creature.

"Are we absolutely certain Langstrom is Man-Bat?" asked Red Robin.

Batman didn't look up from the computer as he said, "It's him. Man-Bat's blood contains human DNA bonded with extracted genetic material from a bat—"

"Wait, I've got it!" interrupted The Flash. "Man-Bat stole Langstrom's pants!"

Nightwing rolled his eyes and sighed.

Batman continued to read from another computer screen, "Dr. Kirk Langstrom, a zoologist with a focus on bats, was rumored to have created a serum to grant humans a bat-like sonar sense to assist the deaf and blind. It was a noble but incredibly experimental idea."

"Do you think he tested it on himself?" asked Nightwing.

"I'm afraid so," replied Batman. "I've analyzed his research, and I think Langstrom was trapped, transformed into Man-Bat. After that happened, Cobblepot gave the creature a place to belong in his Animilitia. Cobblepot only supplied an antidote when he needed Langstrom's scientific expertise."

Batman lifted a vial from a nearby table and said, "And if my calculations are correct, this antidote I've synthesized should return him to human form for three hours."

Batman attached the vial to a small opening in Man-Bat's cell. Soon, a green mist filled the cell, and Man-Bat disappeared within the fog. Only his sharp talons could be seen, now barely scratching at the walls. As the heroes watched in astonishment, Man-Bat's talons were transformed into human fingernails. The fog slowly began to disappear, revealing a middle-aged man. His brown hair was disheveled, and he was wearing only a pair of light-blue pants. It was Kirk Langstrom!

"Amazing!" said Nightwing.

Langstrom looked confused for a moment, studying his surroundings. When he saw the heroes, a sad look came over his face.

"Oh no," he said slowly. "Batman, did I hurt anyone?"

Batman punched a code on a keypad that unlocked the cell, and Langstrom stumbled out, unsteady on his feet. Batman caught him before he fell.

"No, Doctor," he said. "You're under a temporary anti-dote for your condition. If you could help us, perhaps we might be able to make it permanent."

Langstrom looked relieved and said, "I would like nothing more, Batman."

For the next few hours Langstrom and the heroes analyzed the three robotic creatures, methodically taking them apart and then reassembling them. Langstrom patiently explained every last engineering specification of the cyber creatures. Occasionally, Langstrom or one of the heroes would glance at the countdown clock that Batman had activated on the Batcomputer.

Two hours remaining . . .

One hour remaining . . .

Fifteen minutes remaining . . .

Green Arrow extracted a small mechanical device from the Cyber Bat.

"So this is the transmitter?" he asked.

"That's right," said Langstrom. "Cobblepot insisted on being able to communicate directly with the robotic animals."

Batman glanced at the clock. Only eleven minutes left.

"Tell me what you know of Cobblepot's plan," he said.

Langstrom shook his head and said, "Not much, I'm afraid. I was only told to design Cyber Animals for an unmanned exploration and retrieval mission."

Batman looked thoughtful and said, "Retrieval? Like digging through rubble?"

"That's right," said Langstrom.

Batman rushed over to the Batcomputer and pulled up video recordings of the three robberies. First was the jewelry store, with Killer Croc speaking to Cheetah.

"Finish the mission. I'll take care of him," said Croc.

On the next video, Silverback turned to Man-Bat at the bank and said, "Enough. We accomplished what we came for."

On the third video, Silverback called out to the other

members of the Animilitia at the zoo, "Split up and complete the mission!"

Nightwing looked over Batman's shoulder and said, "You were right, Batman. The robberies were just covers!"

Batman's fingers flew over the computer keyboard to create a three-dimensional hologram that showed all twelve robbery sites. In the center of the hologram was the Aviary Building, with its distinctive pointed antenna.

"There's a reason the Aviary is at the center of all the robberies," said Batman, hitting a few more keys. He then drew lines from the top of the Aviary Building that extended down to the sites of the twelve robberies. The image resembled a large umbrella.

"Just like Cobblepot's umbrella!" said Nightwing.

"Or a force field," said Batman. "But why would Cobblepot build a force field around his building?"

Green Arrow leaned in and pointed to the tall antenna atop the Aviary.

"This antenna was clearly built to aim at something," he said.

Nightwing gulped and said, "Something that would require a force field to withstand its massive impact."

"And my robots to pick through the wreckage afterward," said Langstrom nervously.

"I'm not following this," said The Flash with a puzzled look. "What could possibly cause that much destruction?"

Batman hit one more key. An image of the Midas Heart asteroid filled the screen.

"Cobblepot is going to crash the asteroid into Gotham City," he said grimly. "He's going to use the robots to sort through the rubble and retrieve the gold at the center of the asteroid."

"With three robots?" asked Nightwing. "That would take years!"

Langstrom looked pale. He cleared his throat and said quietly, "I'm sorry to say that we did not create just three robots. There are over a thousand Cyber Animals."

BUZZZZ!

The two-minute warning alarm buzzed on the countdown clock. Langstrom's time had run out. Batman reluctantly led the doctor back to the cell.

"Your help has been invaluable, Dr. Langstrom," said Batman. "I hate to do this."

"No, Batman, I understand," said Langstrom sadly. "I want you to lock me up so I can no longer assist Cobblepot."

As Batman walked back to the Batcomputer, Red

Robin whispered to him, "Maybe the antidote will work again?"

Batman shook his head and replied, "No. The serum has already mutated within his body."

"But Langstrom *helped* us!" protested Red Robin. "We can't just leave him locked up!"

The countdown clock beeped for the last five seconds, and then the door of the cell slammed shut, locking with a final click.

Red Robin put his hands on the Plexiglas, and within the cell Langstrom raised his hands. He smiled at Red Robin and said, "It's okay. It's better this way."

A final alarm sounded. Before the horrified eyes of the heroes, Langstrom started thrashing within his cell. First his hands and feet were replaced with furry paws. Then leathery wings erupted from his back. As Langstrom yelled and writhed in pain, his head changed into the giant head of a bat. The transformation was complete.

Man-Bat screeched and angrily banged on the cell walls!

"Come on," said Batman as he led the other heroes out of the Batcave. "We need to get prepared."

Seconds after the heroes departed, the eyes of the

three cyber creatures clicked open and emitted a red glow. All three robots twitched and started to move. The voice of the Penguin was transmitted into their ears.

"Come to me," the voice said. "Come home, my darlings!"

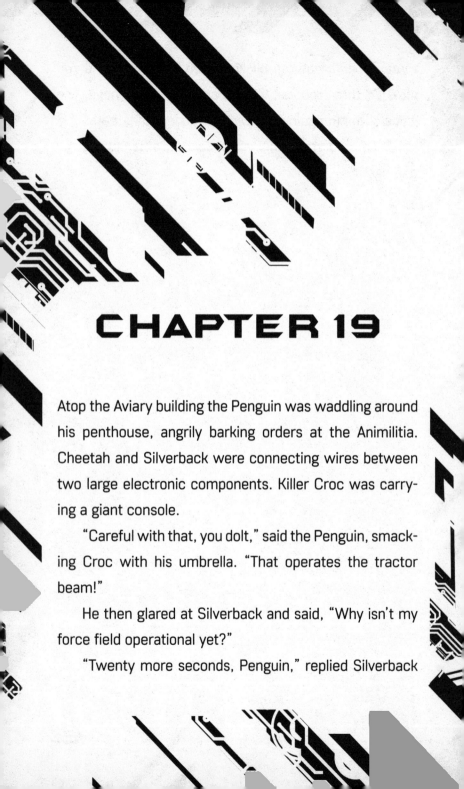

CHAPTER 19

Atop the Aviary building the Penguin was waddling around his penthouse, angrily barking orders at the Animilitia. Cheetah and Silverback were connecting wires between two large electronic components. Killer Croc was carrying a giant console.

"Careful with that, you dolt," said the Penguin, smacking Croc with his umbrella. "That operates the tractor beam!"

He then glared at Silverback and said, "Why isn't my force field operational yet?"

"Twenty more seconds, Penguin," replied Silverback

as he carefully threaded two wires together.

Suddenly, the elevator doors opened. The robotic tiger, wolf, and bat entered the room.

"Ah, my darlings, you've made it home just in time for the big bang and the rain of gold to follow," the Penguin said with a smile. "Go, join your brethren."

The Penguin pressed a button on his umbrella, and a large panel in the wall slid open, revealing a dark room filled with hundreds of Cyber Animals. The three robots marched into the room and joined the other creatures.

Silverback pushed a button on the console, and within seconds it emitted a humming glow of energy.

"It's working!" said Cheetah.

"The tractor beam locked in," said Silverback. "Everything is ready, Mr. Penguin."

As the Penguin hoarsely laughed, a ray of bright red light suddenly shot up into the air from the center of the Gotham City Zoo. While the citizens of Gotham City watched in wonder, similar rays of light crashed through the roofs of the Belle and the Bird jewelry store and the Gotham National Bank, extending into the nighttime sky. Nine other red light beams suddenly rose above the city.

The twelve beams of light all started moving, bending slowly toward the highest spot in Gotham City. With a loud electrical spark, the beams collided on top of the Aviary Building. Then, with a crackle of energy, all twelve pillars of light started to expand, filling in the spaces between them. A huge dome of energy, shaped like an umbrella, surrounded the entire Aviary Building. Only the building's antenna extended above the energy dome.

On the street below, a young man on a bicycle was texting his girlfriend and not looking where he was going.

BLAM!

He slammed into the shimmering red wall of energy and was knocked to the street. A car honked and swerved to avoid hitting the fallen man, and then the car crashed into the red wall.

Above them a police hovercraft bumped up against the wall of energy, unable to proceed.

"What the heck?" said the confused police officer.

The antenna above the Aviary Building began to hum. A tractor beam within the antenna reached out to the orbiting Midas Heart asteroid and slowly began to pull the asteroid out of its orbit.

The Penguin walked over to a window and peered down at Gotham City with disgust. He then grabbed a video camera and began speaking into it. Suddenly, the booming sound of his voice could be heard throughout the entire city.

"Greetings to the pathetic and doomed denizens of Gotham City, who dared to grace me with their sidelong glances, frightened whispers, and withering disrespect."

In downtown Gotham City startled citizens looked up at the dozens of video screens on the buildings. Filling every single screen was the image of Oswald Cobblepot. Flecks of spit sprayed from his mouth as his voice rose and he waved his umbrella angrily.

"I was Oswald Cobblepot," he shouted, "but you may now call me the Penguin! Gather around, everyone. I hope you enjoy the spectacular light show that is about to begin. It is all for you."

The Penguin paused. As an evil grin spread across his face, he added, "Well, it's all for your ultimate *demise*, anyway! Wauk-wauk-wauk!"

The Penguin's voice became louder from the video screens atop Gotham City's buildings.

"My entire life I have been shunned and alienated by you, Gotham," he angrily shouted. "But now *I* will do the shunning! You see, the Midas Heart asteroid is no longer going to harmlessly whiz past the Earth."

As the crowd murmured in disbelief, the Penguin smiled triumphantly.

"I have altered the path of the asteroid with a tractor beam high above my Aviary Building," he said. "And now I will crash the Midas Heart asteroid into Gotham!"

Screams erupted from the crowds below.

"I gotta get out of here," yelled one taxi driver as she swerved her vehicle and knocked over a fire hydrant. Pedestrians tripped over one another, yelling and shoving as they frantically ran away.

"Please don't worry about me," the Penguin said reassuringly. "I'll be safely ensconced behind my red force field. And after you are gone, I will recover the gold at the center of the asteroid and live happily, wealthily, and free of your pathetic judgment. Good-bye, Gotham City. *Forever!*"

With a click, the video screens went dark.

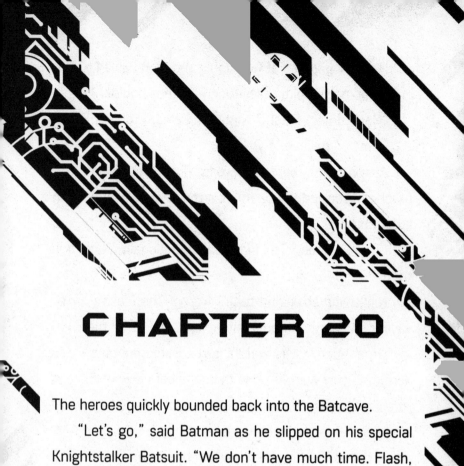

CHAPTER 20

The heroes quickly bounded back into the Batcave.

"Let's go," said Batman as he slipped on his special Knightstalker Batsuit. "We don't have much time. Flash, are you ready?"

"You know, I've never done anything like this before," The Flash said nervously. "I guess I can *try* to vibrate my frequency on a molecular level—"

"But if you screw it up?" interrupted Red Robin. "Going *that* fast? You're going to *splat* against that force field like a bug!"

The Flash gulped nervously.

Nightwing glared at Red Robin and then turned to The Flash and patted him reassuringly on the shoulder.

"Calm down, Flash," Nightwing said. "You can do it. I . . . um . . . believe in you."

A wide grin spread across The Flash's face. He reached over and wrapped his arms around Nightwing in a tight hug.

"Thanks, man," The Flash said emotionally. "I *needed* that!"

Nightwing struggled to get free of The Flash's arms, saying, "All right, c'mon. Just—*please* get off of me."

Green Arrow was watching the Batcomputer's video screens. They were filled with images of panicky citizens running through the streets of Gotham City, which were clogged with abandoned vehicles.

"There's no way you're getting the Batmobile through all that," he said to Batman.

Suddenly, in response to a button that Batman pushed on his Utility Belt, the Batwing roared to life behind them.

"Not a problem," said Batman as he jumped into the flying vehicle. Seconds later, the Batwing was soaring down a tunnel and out of the Batcave. The Flash ran below the Batwing, zipping through the streets of Gotham City.

The Gotham City Police Department had gathered

outside the Aviary Building, with hundreds of police cars circling the red force field. Commissioner Gordon stepped forward and raised a microphone to his mouth.

"This is Commissioner Gordon," he called out, his voice booming through the streets. "We've got your entire building surrounded, Penguin. Give yourself up, or we'll be forced to bust our way in!"

Suddenly, the video screens above the city crackled to life. The leering face of the Penguin appeared on them.

"You are welcome to try, Commissioner," the Penguin said tauntingly. "Go on, give it a shot. I *dare* you!"

Gordon frowned and called out to his police officers, "Open fire!"

ZAP! ZAP! ZAP!

The police fired round after round of laser shots at the wall of red energy, but the blasts bounced harmlessly off the force field.

"You're going to have to do better than *that*," the Penguin said smugly. "My force field was built to withstand a collision with an asteroid."

"You want better?" Gordon muttered to himself. "I'll give you better."

Just then, a massive armored tank rolled closer. Gordon waved to the driver, motioning him to proceed.

"Crack that shield open," he instructed. "We have to get in there!"

BLAM! BLAM!

The tank fired two rockets, but both crumbled into tiny fragments when they hit the red wall.

"Plan B!" called out Gordon.

With a loud rumble, the tank charged right at the force field.

CRASH!

The tank collided with the red wall and was knocked on its side. Huge metal shards of the tank clattered to the ground. The force field continued to glow, undamaged.

A police officer turned to Gordon and asked, "What now, Commissioner?"

Gordon shook his head sadly and said, "I don't know. I just don't know."

WHOOSH!

Suddenly, the Batwing flew past them and came to a halt in front of the force field. Batman hopped out of the vehicle and dropped to the ground. One second later, The Flash zoomed into view and stood next to him.

Gordon approached the two heroes and said, "Batman, we've thrown everything we have against this force field. But nothing gets through."

"I have an idea," replied Batman. "I'm going to walk through it."

Gordon looked doubtful but didn't say anything as Batman activated a button on the chest of his Knight-stalker Batsuit. Sections of the suit began to hum with an electrical glow. Batman walked confidently toward the force field and then slammed his wrists together. A deep red light that was the same color as the force field surrounded his entire suit. Batman struggled to shove his body into the force field, first with his hands and then with his forearms. Exerting all his muscles, he pushed harder and harder until he had walked through the force field!

In the Aviary penthouse the Penguin was watching the action on his video screen. His jaw dropped.

"He can't *do* that!" he screamed with anger. "Batman can't match my shield's frequency. Where did he get a transmitter?"

Suddenly, the Penguin realized what had happened.

"Langstrom must have helped him! Curse that traitor!" he yelled. "Silverback, send down the Cyber Animals!"

Silverback reached for a button on a control panel.

"How many robots?" he asked.

The Penguin gritted his teeth and replied, "*All* of them. I want them to tear Batman apart!"

CHAPTER 21

Just as Batman emerged on the other side of the force field, the doors of the Aviary Building sprang open. Hundreds of roaring cyber creatures charged out of the building, leaping and flying toward Batman.

The Dark Knight quickly shed his Knightstalker Batsuit and fired a grapple that sent him soaring above the snapping jaws of the robotic wolves and tigers. As he zipped through the air, he dodged the laser blasts of the flying Cyber Bats.

Batman spoke into his communicator link, "Flash! Do it now!"

Outside the force field The Flash gulped nervously and started running in place. His feet became a blur of red motion.

"I can do this, I can do this," he muttered to himself as he pumped his arms faster and faster.

Soon, he was zooming toward the red wall of energy, seconds from impact.

BLAM!

The Flash bounced off the force field and landed with a thud on his back.

"Ouch!" he said, rubbing his sore shoulder blades.

Batman was pinned to a wall of the Aviary Building, struggling to avoid the clanking jaws of a Cyber Tiger. Using every muscle in his arms, the Dark Knight managed to avoid the creature's sharp teeth.

"Ace, come!" yelled Batman.

Suddenly, one of the Cyber Wolves came running over to Batman. The creature was covered in black scars, and it stood before the Dark Knight, wagging its mechanical tail. It was the same robotic wolf that had been in the Batcave earlier that evening.

A panel opened up on the wolf's chest, and a giant tire emerged. The creature was transformed into a motor-cycle. Batman jumped onto the machine, just as two other cyber creatures joined him. A robotic bat and tiger both stood alongside Batman, facing down the army of robots.

Watching a video screen in the penthouse above them, the Penguin gasped with astonishment.

"Did you see that?" asked Killer Croc.

"Batman has hacked three of the robots," said Silverback.

"This is *fowl* play," squawked the Penguin. "He has brainwashed my babies!"

The Penguin yelled into a communicator that was linked to the robotic animals.

"Destroy him, my Cyber Children!" he ordered. "Crush him in your pneumatic jaws. Show Batman that he has no place in our animal kingdom!"

Batman yelled into his communicator link, "Flash, it's up to you. Get that shield down!"

Outside the force field The Flash ran a mile down the street. He then turned to face the red wall of energy.

The Flash clenched his fists and started pumping his legs. Soon, he was a blur of red as he accelerated faster than a rocket toward the force field. Sparks flew below him as his feet pounded the streets. The red wall of the force field was getting closer and closer. The Flash panted loudly, running faster than he had ever run before. And then . . .

WHOOOSH!

The Flash collapsed facedown on the ground, breathing heavily. He nervously looked up to see where he was. With a smile, he realized what he had accomplished.

"I made it!" he said happily, "I'm on the other side of the force field!"

Batman zoomed past him on a motorcycle. The Dark Knight was flinging exploding Batarangs at the Cyber Animals that were snapping at his heels.

"Good job, Flash," called out Batman. "Now all you have to do is destroy a receiver at one of the robbery sites and get this shield down!"

A snarling wolf jumped out of the pack of Cyber Animals, reaching for Batman's legs.

"Give me a few minutes to catch my breath!" said The Flash.

Batman swerved to the left and crashed his bike into a wolf.

Just then, four robotic tigers roared into view and started chasing The Flash. As he sped away from the Cyber Animals, he thought to himself, *If I were one of the Penguin's receivers, where would I be?*

He then looked up at the rays of red light above him and said, "Follow the beams, right?"

With the Cyber Tigers hot in pursuit, The Flash ran through the streets of Gotham City and headed toward the Gotham National Bank. A beam of red light was shining from the roof of the bank. The heavy door of the bank was closed, but that wasn't enough to stop The Flash. He accelerated and ran even faster, altering the molecules in his body again to allow him to pass through the door unharmed. The Flash was inside the bank, zipping around and searching for the Penguin's receiver.

CRASH!

The four robotic tigers crashed through the door of the bank, roaring in anger. The Flash sped past one of them, but it quickly extended its metal tail.

"Ugh!" cried The Flash as the tiger's tail grabbed his leg. The Flash then watched in horror as another tiger's tail wrapped itself around his other leg like a tentacle. Another tiger's tail then wrapped around his neck.

"Oh, great, the robots have upgraded," muttered The Flash, frantically pumping his legs, trying to escape. He was now moving very slowly, dragging the three growling metal tigers across the floor of the bank. Just then, he spotted the Penguin's receiver emitting a ray of red light.

The Flash reached out his right hand, desperately struggling to shake the three metallic tails that encased him. The tigers were too strong, though. Slowly, they tugged The Flash away from the receiver. Their jaws opened wider as they pulled The Flash closer and closer.

BLAM!

A fourth robotic tiger slammed into the other three, knocking them against the bank's marble columns. This robot was the hacked tiger from the Batcave!

The Flash jumped to his feet and grabbed the receiver.

"Um, where's the off switch on this?" he wondered, shaking the device. Then he threw it against the ground and stomped on it. It still gave off a red glow.

"Here, boy!" he called out to the hacked Cyber Tiger. "Open wide!"

The creature happily opened its mouth, displaying razor-sharp teeth. The Flash tossed the receiver into the mouth of the tiger, which bit down on the machine and crushed it within its pneumatic jaws.

ZAAAAAP!

"Good kitty," said The Flash as he looked outside the window. The red beams were fading away in the nighttime sky. Within minutes, the entire force field had disappeared!

"Good boy! Good cyber—er—tiger mecha . . . thing?" The Flash said as he patted the head of the tiger. "You need a better nickname, buddy."

The tiger roared in agreement.

CHAPTER 22

Back in the Batcave, Red Robin watched on a video screen as the force field disappeared.

"Yes!" he yelled, pumping his fist in the air. "The shield is down. Uploading now."

BLAM! BLAM!

Man-Bat struggled within the Plexiglas cell behind Red Robin. In all the excitement, Red Robin had failed to notice that a hairline crack now appeared within the Plexiglas. As Man-Bat continued to pound on the wall, the crack slowly grew wider.

"Now that the shield is down, I'm going into the

Aviary," announced Batman. "Red Robin, let me know as soon as that upload is completed!"

Outside the Aviary Building, Batman fired a grapple and jumped over a snarling pack of Cyber Wolves. A Cyber Bat came swooping around the building, firing lasers at the Dark Knight.

WHAM!

Green Arrow had joined the fight and shot an exploding arrow at the robotic bat, knocking the creature out of the air. "Don't worry, Bats," he said. "We've got your back."

ZAP! ZAP!

With the force field eliminated, Commissioner Gordon and the Gotham City Police Department now surrounded the Aviary, firing their lasers at the Cyber Animals. Two Cyber Bats crashed to the ground.

Nightwing jumped off the Batcycle and rammed a Cyber Wolf with his electrical batons. But the cyber creatures just kept coming!

"Where are we with the upload?" Batman yelled into his communicator.

"Over halfway," reported Red Robin. "Sixty-five percent!"

In the Aviary penthouse the Penguin was frantically

pushing buttons on the computer console.

"No, this can't be!" yelled the Penguin. "My console has gone dark! I can't turn off the tractor beam!"

The three members of the Animilitia exchanged worried glances.

"But—the asteroid . . . ," Cheetah said nervously. "It's still headed right for this building."

"And without the force field to protect us . . . ," came Killer Croc.

Silverback did a quick mental calculation and said, "Our survival probability is at exactly zero-point-zero percent."

The Penguin started slowly backing out of the room, discreetly heading toward an elevator door.

"Well, that's my cue to exit, I believe," he said, taking a deep bow. "Trust me, it's been a thin slice of heaven working with each of you."

"Wait, wh-what?" Cheetah sputtered. "Where are you going?"

As the Penguin stepped into the open elevator, he said, "I would take you with me, but, silly me, I only built this escape pod for *one*. I bid you adieu."

The Penguin tapped a button inside the elevator with his umbrella, and the giant steel door slammed shut.

The Animilitia jumped up and ran to the metal door, pounding on it and shouting.

"Cobblepot, open this door!" yelled Killer Croc.

"Take me! Please, take me with you!" pleaded Cheetah.

WHOOSH!

Flames shot out from rocket blasters below the elevator pod, and it rapidly accelerated, crashing through the roof of the Aviary Building. Within seconds the Penguin was soaring through the sky, sailing far away from Gotham City.

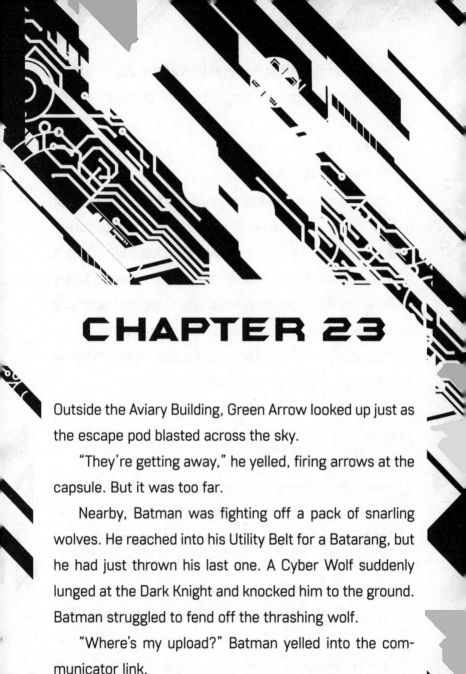

CHAPTER 23

Outside the Aviary Building, Green Arrow looked up just as the escape pod blasted across the sky.

"They're getting away," he yelled, firing arrows at the capsule. But it was too far.

Nearby, Batman was fighting off a pack of snarling wolves. He reached into his Utility Belt for a Batarang, but he had just thrown his last one. A Cyber Wolf suddenly lunged at the Dark Knight and knocked him to the ground. Batman struggled to fend off the thrashing wolf.

"Where's my upload?" Batman yelled into the communicator link.

In the Batcave, Red Robin stared at the status bar on the computer screen: 98 percent . . . 99 percent . . . And then . . .

DING!

"It's done!" Red Robin exclaimed.

Batman slowly released his hands from the jaws of the wolf, which had instantly gone slack. The cyber creature lurched to its feet and swayed unsteadily. Then it fell to the ground with a loud crash. All around the Aviary Building the hundreds of robotic tigers, wolves, and bats all crashed to the ground and lay there, unmoving.

"Langstrom's computer virus worked," Batman spoke into the communicator. "The robots are down."

In the Batcave, Red Robin leaned back in his chair, satisfied with a job well done.

SMASH!

Red Robin spun around to discover that Man-Bat had broken out of his cell! The creature's bloodred eyes glared at Red Robin, and it slowly unfurled its leathery wings.

"Aw, no," muttered Red Robin as he jumped over a chair to land in front of Man-Bat.

"Please, Dr. Langstrom," he pleaded. "I *know* you! You know *me*!"

Man-Bat hesitated for a moment and cocked his head.

He was staring intently at Red Robin.

"Dr. Langstrom," continued Red Robin, "I know you can hear me. We're trying to help you!"

Man-Bat opened his mouth wide, as if he was trying to speak. But instead of a human voice, a violent animal scream erupted from his throat. With an enraged look on his face, Man-Bat tried to knock Red Robin aside with his wing.

Red Robin executed a perfect backflip and then catapulted forward, landing on Man-Bat's back. The creature struggled to shake Red Robin loose.

"I'm sorry, Doctor. I can't let you do this."

Suddenly, Man-Bat spread his wings and leaped in the air. Soon, he was zooming through the tunnel, out of the Batcave, and flying high above Gotham City, with Red Robin holding on tight.

"Please, Dr. Langstrom," he said into Man-Bat's ear. "Your body has changed, but not your mind. Please concentrate. We need your help!"

Man-Bat's face contorted, momentarily seeming to consider what the young hero was saying. Then the creature growled and flipped upside down, sending Red Robin plummeting to the ground.

As Man-Bat watched the hero fall, a change came

over the creature's face. His eyes widened, and he suddenly looked sad. Red Robin was going to be hurt—badly,
and it was going to be his fault. Man-Bat spread his wings
and went into a dive, scooping up Red Robin in midair,
seconds before he would have hit the ground.

"Dr. Langstrom?" said a very relieved Red Robin.

The creature nodded his head.

"I *knew* you could do it," Red Robin said with a smile.
"Let's get to the others!"

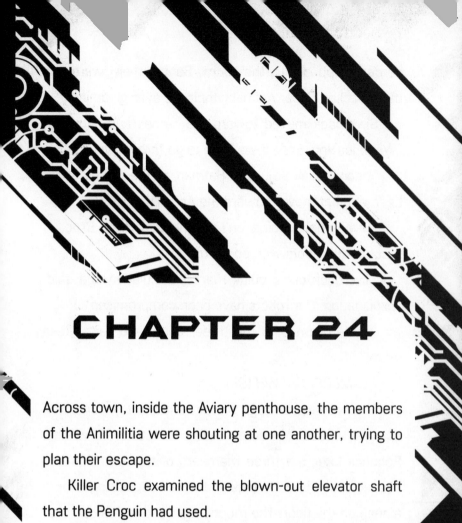

CHAPTER 24

Across town, inside the Aviary penthouse, the members of the Animilitia were shouting at one another, trying to plan their escape.

Killer Croc examined the blown-out elevator shaft that the Penguin had used.

"We ain't going this way," he said with a growl.

"We've got to get out of here!" Cheetah screamed. She frantically pushed the button for the only other elevator in the penthouse.

DING!

The elevator door opened, and Batman and the other

heroes stepped into the room. Behind them were the three hacked Cyber Animals, their red eyes gleaming.

Silverback moved toward the heroes and declared, "We're leaving. Even if we have to go *through* you."

"I don't think so," said Batman as the robotic wolf, tiger, and bat moved toward the Animilitia.

"Hey, what's going on?" demanded Killer Croc. "I thought the robots worked for *us*!"

Silverback did a quick mental calculation and said, "Explanation: Our robots have been compromised."

Batman turned to the three robots and said, "Take them!"

BLAM! CRASH! WHACK!

The bat flew through the air, and the tiger and wolf charged across the room, landing on top of the villains. Seconds later the three members of the Animilitia had been knocked unconscious and were huddled together in a heap on the floor. The robotic tiger and wolf stood over them and wagged their tails happily.

Green Arrow turned to the other heroes and said, "So the bad guys are down, but what about the giant flaming rock?"

"Can we reverse the polarity of that tractor beam?" Nightwing asked.

Batman studied the computer console for a few moments and then shook his head.

"I could, but the controls are blown out," he said. "I don't have the parts to repair it."

Red Robin consulted his Bat-tablet and announced, "The Midas Heart asteroid is due to arrive in twelve minutes."

"I have an idea," said Batman. "Arrow, I need you to find a new power source for the console."

"On it," said Green Arrow.

Batman continued, "Flash and Nightwing, I need you to collect parts. Nightwing knows what I need. Flash, you help him get it quickly."

Nightwing and The Flash zipped from the room. Green Arrow gathered the machine's power cord, and Batman threw an exploding Batarang at the window.

BLAM!

Batman ran to the shattered window, fired a grapple line, and swung out of the building, calling out to the other heroes, "I'm going to rewire the junction box for the antenna."

Seconds later The Flash returned to the room, carrying one of the Penguin's receivers and pieces of a Cyber Tiger. Nightwing grabbed the devices and popped them open.

"This should work," he said as he pried open the receiver and started moving wires within it.

"The power is back on," Green Arrow said proudly as the console hummed to life.

"How did you get the power back on?" asked Nightwing.

Green Arrow pointed to the unconscious Silverback in the corner. The power cable was now connected to Silverback's energy panel. The giant ape was powering the console.

Nightwing carried the receiver-turned-transmitter to the window and leaned out. Batman was precariously balanced on a ledge, calmly rewiring the junction box.

"This transmitter should work, Batman," said Nightwing. "But how do we get it up above the antenna?"

Suddenly, Man-Bat and Red Robin swooped through the open window and landed in the penthouse.

"Maybe Man-Bat can help with that," said Red Robin.

"Flash, you're not done," called out Batman. "I need you to collect the other receivers. Then I want you to place them at equal distances along the edges of Gotham City."

"Gotcha," said The Flash, zipping out of the building.

The streets of Gotham City were clogged with debris and abandoned cars, but The Flash expertly dodged each obstacle, moving so fast that he became a red streak zooming through the city. Within minutes all eleven receivers had been placed in a circle around the outskirts of Gotham City. He then raced back to the Aviary Building.

Batman continued to work on the junction box as Man-Bat hovered near him.

"Are you certain, Doctor?" asked Batman. "You'll have to fly above the antenna in order to focus the signal. It's going to be dangerous."

Man-Bat nodded his head and took the transmitter from Nightwing's hands. Man-Bat flew to the top of the Aviary Building and then soared even higher, hovering above the building's antenna. In the distance the Midas Heart asteroid could be seen streaking toward Gotham City.

Batman spliced two wires in the junction box and spoke into his communicator, "Arrow? Are you ready?"

Green Arrow turned a knob on the console and said, "The levels are good, Bats. So this is going shoot that asteroid back into space?"

"No," replied Batman. "It's going to pull it *toward* us even faster."

Green Arrow looked up from the machine and exclaimed, "Wait, *what*?!"

Batman continued to connect wires and spoke into

his communicator, "We don't have time to reverse the asteroid's trajectory. But I'm rewiring the force field, and The Flash has moved the receivers. If my calculations are correct, we should be safe."

Green Arrow and The Flash gave each other worried looks.

"And if they aren't?" asked Green Arrow.

"They *are*," said Batman gruffly.

BZZZZZZZ!

As Man-Bat hovered above the antenna atop the Aviary Building, the transmitter in his hands began to hum. A green glow of energy appeared around the transmitter. That same green glow slowly surrounded Man-Bat's hands and the antenna as well. The creature struggled to stay aloft as green energy bursts pulsed through his body.

"Aaaagh!" Man-Bat cried out in pain as he clutched the transmitter close to his chest.

The glowing bursts of energy slowly expanded, covering Man-Bat's entire body and shooting out green beams of light to the eleven receivers at the edge of Gotham City. As each beam of light connected to a receiver, it formed a force field around the entire city. A massive green dome now covered all of Gotham City. The Midas

Heart asteroid picked up speed and plummeted even faster toward the city.

Batman yelled into his communicator, "It's working, Doctor! Just a few more minutes!"

Man-Bat was about to lose consciousness, but he fought to stay awake as he hovered next to the antenna. The asteroid burst into flames as it entered the Earth's atmosphere. It was heading right for the Aviary Building.

"C'mon, Doc, you can do it!" called out Red Robin.

Green Arrow consulted the console and announced, "Brace for impact! Here it comes!"

The Flash nervously paced the room at superspeed, zooming from one corner to the other, and said, "Oh man, I can't look!"

KER-BLAM!

The sound of a huge explosion filled the room. The building rocked on its foundation as the asteroid crashed into the green force field. A massive power surge knocked out the console and threw the heroes to the floor as the asteroid shattered into fragments that came cascading down outside the force field.

Then there was silence.

Batman ran to the window and watched the debris from the asteroid fall harmlessly into Gotham Harbor. The force field had held! In the streets of Gotham City below he could hear the sound of the crowds cheering with happiness.

Batman then looked up and watched with horror as Man-Bat faltered in the air and started falling. The Dark Knight quickly shot a grapple line that encircled Man-Bat and brought him to safety within the penthouse.

Man-Bat was sprawled on the floor, still clutching the transmitter, which continued to glow green and send energy blasts coursing through his body. As the heroes watched in astonishment, Man-Bat's wings began to shrink. His furry paws morphed into human hands and feet. As the green energy glow faded, he was transformed back into Dr. Langstrom. Slowly, he sat up and blinked his eyes.

"What happened?" he asked. "Did we win?"

Batman leaned over him and put a reassuring hand on Langstrom's shoulder.

"Gotham City owes you a debt of gratitude, Doctor," he said. "We *did* win, thanks to you."

Batman reached into his Utility Belt and removed a medical scanning device, which he passed over Langstrom's body.

"Good news, Doctor," said Batman as he looked at

the device. "It looks as if the tractor beam's power surge burnt out all traces of the bat serum in your blood. If this data is correct, you won't be seeing the Man-Bat again."

Langstrom was overcome with emotion. He grasped Batman's hand and turned to look at the heroes, "Thank you, Batman. Thank you all for giving me my life back!"

Red Robin and Nightwing had looped titanium rope around the members of the Animilitia, who were groaning in pain. Commissioner Gordon and a dozen police officers marched the Animilitia out of the Aviary Building, ready to escort the villains back to Arkham Asylum.

"You can't keep me locked up like some kind of *animal*," grumbled Cheetah as she was pushed into the police van.

Killer Croc moaned and said, "I hate prison. The food is terrible. And the portions are so *tiny*!"

Silverback glared at Batman and said, "You haven't seen the last of us, Batman."

Gordon grinned as the door of the police van slammed shut, and he turned around to look at Batman. But the Dark Knight had disappeared.

Standing on a rooftop not far from the Aviary Building, the heroes watched the police van drive away.

The Flash tried to place his hand on Nightwing's shoulder, but Nightwing shifted his body out of the way.

"So, thanks, and stuff," said The Flash. "You know, for believing in me."

"Yeah, it's cool," said Nightwing awkwardly.

"We'll have to do it again," said The Flash.

"Sure, whenever."

"Because I really—" The Flash continued.

"Dude, for the fastest guy, you give the *slowest* good-byes!"

The Flash smiled and took off for his home in Central City. Nightwing dived from the rooftop.

Red Robin was balancing happily on top of the hacked Cyber Bat. He sailed over to Batman.

"Race you home!" he said.

As The Flash, Red Robin, and Nightwing departed, Green Arrow turned to the Dark Knight and said, "Well, see you around, Bats. Never a dull moment in Gotham City."

Green Arrow fired a grappling arrow. As he sailed into the air, he said, "It's just a shame that the Penguin got away."

Batman just smiled. And then he disappeared into the shadows.

CHAPTER 25

Over nine thousand miles away from Gotham City, a lonely figure waddled through the bleak and chilly expanse of Antarctica. It was the Penguin, muttering and squawking as he slowly trudged through the drifting snow. An icy blast of wind knocked him over, sending his top hat flying through the air. He painfully clambered to his feet and chased after his hat. Nearby, his escape pod lay half-buried in the snow, cracked into pieces. A thick stream of black smoke rose from it.

"Greek Islands . . . bah!" he said as he glared at the damaged escape pod. "Nothing ever works like it's supposed to. Miserable guidance system . . ."

He paused and peered into the pod's exposed machinery. There was a shiny green arrow lodged in the middle of the machine's inner circuits.

The Penguin angrily waddled around the escape pod, kicking it and knocking it with his umbrella.

"Stupid machine!" he yelled. "Stupid Batman! Stupid—"

The Penguin looked up with surprise. Something was moving in the distance. It was moving toward him! Someone was coming to his rescue!

"Over here! Over here! Wauk-wauk-wauk!" he yelled and squawked.

The air was suddenly filled with squawking. The Penguin was puzzled. Was it an echo?

"Wauk-wauk-wauk!" came the sounds.

The Penguin's eyes widened in horror, and his mouth dropped. Coming toward him were hundreds—no, thousands—of penguins. Their wings were spread, and they squawked with happiness as they waddled toward him.

"No, no!" yelled the Penguin, backing away from the approaching birds. "Stay away. Leave me alone! Have you no sense of personal space?!"

But the birds kept coming. One hopped up on his shoulder. Another burrowed deeply into the pockets of his coat. Another crawled atop his head and nestled under his top hat. As the Penguin continued to scream in anguish, more and more birds surrounded him. All were happy to welcome a fellow penguin to his new, and permanent, chilly home.

"I'll get you, Batman!"